Tell the moon to come out

Joan Lingard was born in Edinburgh but grew up in Belfast. She finds inspiration for her books from the places she has lived and experienced. *Across the Barricades* was set in Northern Ireland. *Tug of War* in Latvia and *Between Two Worlds* in Canada. She says 'Background and inheritance are very important to me in my writing. My characters are shaped by the environment they have been born into or are growing up in.'

Joan began writing when she was eleven years old and she wanted to be a novelist from that day on.

TELL THE MOON TO COME OUT

JOAN LINGARD

Heinemann

Inspiring generations

Heinemann Educational Publishers
Halley Court, Jordan Hill, Oxford OX2 8EJ
Part of Harcourt Education

Heinemann is the registered trademark of
Harcourt Education Limited

© Joan Lingard 2003

First published in Great Britain in 2003 by the Penguin Group
First published in the New Windmills Series 2005

1

British Library Cataloguing in Publication Data is available
from the British Library on request.

ISBN 0 435 13104 4

Cover illustration by David Dean
Cover design by Words and Publications
Typeset by ✱Tek-Art, Croydon, Surrey

Printed and bound in the United Kingdom by Clays Ltd, St Ives plc

For Angie and Catriona

Tell the moon to come out
for I do not want to see the blood
of Ignacio on the sand

'Lament for Ignacio Sánchez Mejías'
by Frederico García Lorca (1898–1936)

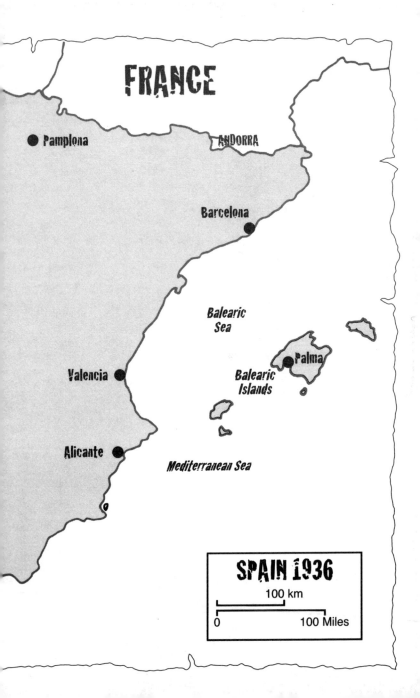

One

He waited in the shelter of the doorway, watching the needle-fine rain fall on the dark street. The night was warm, and humid, and he was sweating in his thick pullover. But he would need it later. Jean-Luc had warned him that it would be cold on the mountain tops even though it was nearing the end of May.

A quiet footfall made him turn his head. Jean-Luc was approaching.

'Nicolás, are you ready?'

Nick nodded.

'You're sure you want to do this?'

'Sure.'

'OK then, let's go. You have your haversack and your water-bottle and your bedroll?'

'Yes.'

Jean-Luc led the way and Nick moved out from the doorway, feeling the rain soft on his face. They kept close to the walls. Only a few windows were lit. This was a mountain village where people rose early and retired early. His mother had gone to bed an hour ago. He hoped she would be sleeping soundly. Since his father had gone she seldom had. He hoped, too, that she would not wake before morning. He had left her a note on the kitchen table.

Don't worry about me, he had written, *I have to go.* She would worry, of course.

As soon as they left the last house behind, they were climbing. The night seemed blacker now, with only a few faint blinks of light showing in the valley below. His legs were strong from climbing in the Scottish hills and he knew how to pace himself. Before long, though, his lungs were labouring, for these Pyrenean slopes were steep, and his breathing had become short and rasping. Ahead of him Jean-Luc moved with the agility of one of his own mountain goats. He looked back and waited on top of a small knoll.

Nick stopped, too, for a moment and took a small swig from his water-bottle; and by the time they set off again he had found his second wind and could keep up with Jean-Luc. The rain had petered out but there was no sign of the moon that was up there somewhere behind the heavy banks of cloud. Now that his eyes had adjusted, he was able to make out the dark shapes of overhanging rocks and a few stunted trees bent by fierce winds. They were following a smugglers' trail that Jean-Luc knew well. He had helped many men – Nick's father among them – to cross from France into Spain to fight for the Republican cause in the Civil War.

As they neared the summit a wind close to gale-force sprang up, tearing at their clothes and whipping their hair across their faces. They walked bent over, like half-shut penknives, trying to keep as close to the ground as possible. At times they had to drop on to their hands and knees to avoid being blown over.

Finally, they reached the summit. Nick felt as if he were standing on top of the world, surrounded by vast stretches of darkness. The unknown. The wind was even fiercer here.

Jean-Luc put an arm round his shoulder. 'Keep going down,' he shouted into Nick's ear. 'Remember all the things I've told you!'

Nick nodded. His head was packed full of information, of routes to take, places to avoid, names of people, contacts who would help him. 'Thank you, Jean-Luc,' he said, but his words were lost on the wind.

Jean-Luc grasped his hand and then turned and began making his way back down the mountain on the French side. When the top of his head disappeared Nick felt fear and doubt grip him for the first time. He squatted down on to his hunkers and lowered his head. What was he doing out here in this wilderness all by himself? Was he mad to have set out? The wind was like a maniac, roaring and howling. Were there wolves on these mountains? He thought it possible, though he was sure that he'd heard that wolves seldom attacked people. His throat contracted and his tongue felt thick and dry. He took another small mouthful from his water-bottle, knowing he could not afford to gulp. His water ration was precious.

He had to take a grip of himself. He had to go on, to try to find out what had happened to his father. When the defeated Republican soldiers had come straggling back to France in the spring his father had not been among them. None of the men knew whether or not he had died in any of the terrible battles that had decimated their ranks. The Nationalists, led by General Franco, having won the war, were now in control of the country. Nick braced himself and, pushing up on to his feet, began his descent into Spain.

He went cautiously, shining his torch only occasionally, taking care to keep the light angled downward. Not that it seemed likely anyone else would be up here at this time of night, but one never knew. *Assume nothing*, Jean-Luc had told him. *Make it your motto.* Nick's head buzzed with all the things he'd been told.

From time to time he rested and when he did he listened, in the way that a deer in the forest might, with its head cocked, ears pricked, ready at the slightest sign of danger to spring away through the trees making the merest whisper of sound. He wished he could move as swiftly and lightly. He felt clumsy, stumbling over unseen

3

rocks. His progress was slow and the night was long. He was relieved when the darkness began to ebb and a vague outline of the terrain became visible.

When he came to a pine forest he plunged gratefully into it. Here he had cover. Here he could relax a little. The paths underfoot were soft with fallen pine needles. The smell of the pines made him think of Scotland, of the Inverness-shire glen where he lived with his mother, and had lived with his father until the autumn of 1936, nearly three years ago. He remembered the moment his father had come into the kitchen and made his announcement.

'I'm going to Spain.' His dark eyes had had a faraway look in them. It was as if he had already gone. 'I have to go. It's my country and it's in trouble. And my family is there.'

Nick's mother had risen from the table and was standing with her hands clasped in front of her. She had been afraid of this ever since summer, when they had heard the first reports of the fighting. Her voice when she spoke was low. 'We are your family, too, Sebastián.'

'Of course you are! And you are more important to me than anything else in the world. But you are safe here. Scotland is not being torn apart, the way Spain is.'

'Yes, you must go, I realise that,' said Nick's mother sadly.

That night Nick's father came into his room and sat on the edge of his bed. 'You do understand why I'm going, don't you, son?'

Nick nodded, not trusting himself to speak. Then he burst out, 'But I still wish you didn't have to go! I'll miss you, Dad.'

'And I'll miss you, Nicolás.' His father engulfed him in his arms and they held on to each other tightly. 'I'll be back, I promise you.'

But he had not come back and Nick knew that such a promise might not have been within his father's power to keep.

4

As he emerged from the trees he heard the sound of ferocious growling. Two wild dogs with long yellow fangs were tearing at the carcass of another animal. A deer perhaps. Nick smelt blood and rotting flesh and his stomach churned, bringing a taste of bile up into his throat. Sensing his presence, the dogs lifted their heads and stared at him with red, flaring eyes. He resisted the impulse to turn and flee and after a moment they went back, snarling and growling, to their prey. He made a wide detour round them.

When next he glanced up he saw a thin line of scarlet in the eastern sky. Light was gradually seeping on to the land. Before him stretched rolling countryside, swathes of forest, fields where sheep grazed, with a few houses dotted here and there. It was a peaceful enough scene, though he knew that could be deceptive. He had been well primed not only by Jean-Luc but by Spanish veterans of the Civil War who had sought refuge in France and were now living in camps across the border from their homeland. Nick had spent the last two months talking to them, listening to their stories, gathering information that would help him on his journey. They had not encouraged him to make it; they had warned him he would be going into enemy territory. *If Franco's men catch you*, they had told him, *they will show no mercy*. They were still hunting down soldiers from the Republican side, imprisoning and, in some cases, shooting them without further ado. It had been a bitter war, with terrible atrocities committed on both sides, brother sometimes fighting against brother.

But the dawn was beautiful. The sun was coming up fast, sending streaks of pink, turquoise and pale yellow across the sky. The birds were in full noisy song, while the rest of the world stayed quiet. He could not linger; he must track down his first contact as soon as

5

possible. He crossed a field and, skirting a scraggy wood, reached a road. It must be the road running south to Pamplona.

He was in Spain.

Two

Nick was about to cross the road when he heard a vehicle. He ducked behind a small thicket and watched as a dusty greyish van came into sight. It pulled up on the road just a few yards short of him. A door swung open on either side of the van and out sprang two men wearing grey-green uniforms and patent-leather three-cornered hats. Nick recognised immediately the uniform of the Guardia Civil, the Civil Guard – a paramilitary organisation which exercised considerable power and was much feared. The veterans in the camps had spoken a great deal about it. Many had suffered from its brutality. *Avoid it if you can*, he had been advised. At the beginning of the war the Guard had been split, some of its members supporting the Nationalists and Franco, others the Republicans. Any guards around now would be Franco supporters.

One of the guards had a rifle slung over his shoulder. Nick wondered if they could have been watching from further along the road and had seen him on the hill. He had no identity papers; for that alone they could arrest him. Imagine if he were to be arrested so soon after arriving in Spain!

The two guards, however, appeared not to be interested in anything in particular. They were stretching themselves as if they had been driving for a long time. They lit cigarettes. They took turns to drink from a water-bottle. The one with the rifle came sauntering up the road in Nick's direction and stopped right in front of the thicket. He heard the man belch. He himself was hardly daring to breathe.

Then he heard the sound of another engine. A moment or two later, a beaten-up old van of indecipherable colour came clanking into view and was flagged down by the guards. The driver, a small elderly man in shabby blue overalls and a cap, was ordered to get out. The armed guard poked him in the ribs with his rifle and told him to hurry, hurry, they didn't have all day to waste, they had more important things to do. They demanded his papers and became impatient as he fumbled in his pocket. They examined them, returned them, and then told the old man to open up the back of his van. He was reluctant; the rifle poked him again. He opened the back door. The unarmed guard pushed him out of the way and, reaching into the interior of the van, withdrew a dead, unplucked chicken. He held it up by its legs and swung it to and fro, its feathered head almost grazing the ground. The van driver was quivering.

Suddenly he found his voice. It was high and reedy. 'You're not going to take my chicken! My family's starving. My grandchildren have had nothing but bread for a week.'

'Where did you get it, old man? We'll wager you stole it.' The chicken went on swinging to and fro, to and fro, the eyes of the three men following it. 'Come now, own up!'

'This will make us a good dinner at the station tonight, Alfonso.' The armed guard laughed.

'You can't do that!' The old man reached out to take the bird but was pushed back roughly.

'You'll not tell us what to do!'

'My son fought on your side. He died at the battle of Jarama.'

'Then you should feel honoured, old man, that your son died for a noble cause. Get back in your old wreck! You're lucky. If it was any good we'd have it for ourselves.'

The old man climbed back into the driver's seat but made no effort to start the engine. He sat with his head slumped forward.

Laughing, the two guards strolled back to their vehicle and threw the chicken into it. Then they drove off, blaring their horn at the old man as they passed. Nick wished he could go over and speak to him but, of course, he dared not. Besides, the old man's son had fought on the opposite side to his own father, for the Fascist Nationalists. He had been an enemy of his father.

After a few minutes the old man roused himself and started the van's engine. It coughed and spluttered several times before the van lurched off with black smoke puffing from the exhaust. When Nick could no longer hear it he stood up and eased the crick in his knees. The road was empty again. The sun was fully out now and the day promised to be hot.

When he started to walk he found he was staggering a little. He was tired and had eaten little during the night, only a crust or two of bread. Some solid food and a good sleep and he would be fit to continue his journey. He kept close in to the verge, keeping an eye open for places to hide if a car came. Jean-Luc had said traffic should be light early in the morning, but there was a good chance that what there was would be either army or Civil Guard. Few ordinary people could afford cars. And most had been requisitioned during the war. A farmer standing in a field turned to stare at him but said nothing. *People are suspicious of each other*, he had been told over and over again, *that is what the war has done to people. Before, they would chat, call out greetings, invite a stranger into their home.*

Nick knew exactly what to look for; he'd been given precise instructions. And here was the narrow beaten-earth path at the side of a forked clump of oak trees, with a couple of pigs rooting underneath for acorns. Acorns made good pork, he seemed to remember. He never thought that he would actually find the path. After glancing round to check no one was watching, he turned off the road. The path snaked its way over rough land, then through a small beech wood until, finally, he saw a low stone dwelling ahead.

He approached the house cautiously, his feet making little sound on the earth. Pieces of rusted, tangled farm machinery lay beside the back wall and the shutters were closed over the two small windows at the front and rear. It did not look like a house that was inhabited. He stood still and listened. Not a sound came from within. Perhaps the owner – Francisco – would no longer be there. He might have been taken away by the Civil Guard. He might be dead. The information that the war veterans had was not up to date; they had had no communication with anyone in Spain since leaving two or three months ago. They were afraid to write letters to families left behind in case that would bring trouble to them.

Nick went up to the front door and knocked gently, giving three short knocks and two longer ones. He waited. Then he knocked again, more loudly, and this time he thought he heard a slight movement within. He put his mouth to the crack of the door and spoke.

'My name is Nicolás Torres,' he said. 'I am the son of Sebastián Torres. I have been told to come here by your old friend Paco Gonzales who is now in a refugee camp in France.

Another wait, but this time he definitely heard someone moving on the other side of the door. A bolt rattled, and then the door was opened. A man with longish, wild black hair stood on the threshold, keeping hold of the door's edge. He stared at Nick for a few seconds before coming to life and opening his arms to embrace him.

'I can see that you are the son of Sebastián. You look like him. We fought together, your father and I. You are most welcome, Nicolás. Your father spoke of you, often. Come in, please.'

It was dark inside. They went into a low, almost bare room. A single sputtering candle sent strange shadows over the walls. Lighting a second one, Francisco set it on a wooden table.

'Sit down, lad. You need food, I think?'

'If you can spare any.'

'What I have I will happily share with you.'

From a wall cupboard Francisco produced a half-loaf of greyish bread, a hunk of yellow cheese, a jug of water and a flagon of red wine. He sat down opposite Nick. In the candlelight Nick saw the long puckered scar that snaked from beneath his chin down his neck, before disappearing under his coarse blue shirt. Francisco, seeing him looking, ran his finger down the scar.

'Someone wanted to cut my throat!' He laughed. 'But they did not succeed. If they had I would not be sitting here at this table with you. So, come on, eat, please!' He poured equal measures of wine and water into a mug and passed it across the table. 'And drink! You look drained.'

Nick drank. Even with the added water the wine tasted rough, but it felt good to his parched throat and without it the dry bread and hard cheese would have been difficult to swallow.

'You speak Spanish like a native, Nicolás.'

'I grew up bilingual.'

'You look like one of us! You've been in Spain before?'

'The south only. Andalusia. Where my father's parents live. We visited them a few times. Before 1936.'

'Ah, before 1936. The eighteenth of July. The day our lives changed. When General Franco decided to stage a revolution.'

'So you fought with my father?'

'I did, yes.'

'Is he—' Nick hesitated, almost not daring to put his question, so afraid was he of the answer. 'Do you know if he is still alive?'

Francisco shook his head. 'I don't, Nicolás. The last time I saw him was at the battle of Jarama. But I heard later that he had been at Teruel. Another bloody battle. All battles are bloody! Never be persuaded otherwise. A friend of mine was at Teruel with Sebastián.'

'This friend – does he live near by?'

'No, many kilometres away from here.'

'Can you give me his address?'

'So you've come to look for your father, is that it? You do realise how dangerous that is going to be, don't you? No, you probably don't. How could you?'

'I'll be careful.'

'It's not a case of being careful. For a start, you won't know who you can trust and who you can't.'

'I *must* go.'

Francisco sighed. 'I presume you have no identity papers?'

'Jean-Luc said you might know someone who could help with that?'

'This same friend might, if the Civil Guard hasn't taken him. But now I think you need to sleep?'

Nick did not deny it. Francisco took him into an adjoining room and showed him a pallet of straw. Nick unrolled his bedroll and placed it on top. Then he dropped down on to it and slept.

He dreamt that he was still up on the mountain and that the two wild dogs were sitting on a crag above him, looking down. He saw their red eyes, their yellow teeth. He heard their low, throaty growls. And then they were upon him, trying to tear his flesh to pieces, as he had seen them do to their prey.

'It's all right, lad,' said Francisco.

Nick jerked upright, wondering where he was. Francisco was squatting on the floor beside him. He patted his shoulder.

'You were having a nightmare. That's nothing. We all have those. Now go back to sleep and think how the world looks in the early morning when everything is clean and fresh and unmarked.'

Nick slept again and this time he did not dream or, if he did, he remembered nothing. He slept throughout that day and the night that followed and woke to find another fresh dawn. By then he was ready to press on again.

Three

Nick reached the village as dusk was falling. Francisco had thought it better that he travel by day; at night it might seem suspicious if he were to be seen on the roads. Wherever possible he had cut across meadows and through woods, avoiding the highways where the trucks of the army and the Civil Guard were much in evidence. On one occasion, crossing from one field into another, he had had to scale a high, barbed-wire fence and had snagged his hand, tearing a lump of skin out of the palm. He had wrapped a handkerchief round it and it had stopped bleeding, though it was still painful.

He stopped at the entrance to the village and waited in the shadows. He was learning to wait and listen, not to rush on. He could hear Jean-Luc's voice in his head: You never know when a guard might be round the corner. Keep that thought in mind all the time.

After a moment, Nick began to move again, glad that the light was fading. It was much darker within the narrow streets of the village than it had been out in the open fields. There were no street lamps, though a half-moon gave some light. He saw that a number of the terraced houses had been wrecked, shelled probably during the war. The rubble lay uncleared. Something scuttled across his path. A rat, he thought.

The village was spread out in a long straggly line with one main street – Calle Real, Royal Street – and a number of shorter ones running off it. Francisco had drawn a plan for him before he left and he had fixed it in his head. No paper must be found on him if he were caught. Any information he gave could mean arrest, possibly death, for anyone who helped him.

Water was trickling down the middle of the street. He swerved round a small child playing in it with a tin can. The child did not even glance up at him. A little further on a low bridge spanned a stream, or a burn, as they would have called it back home. On the bridge two girls were filling jugs with water from a fountain.They did look at him. They stared but said nothing. He passed on by, keeping his eyes averted. The only other person abroad was an elderly man walking his dog.

Halfway down the street Nick came upon the sign he was looking for: Calle de la Iglesia. Church Street. And there on the corner, gleaming in the pale light, was the small white church that had given the street its name. The walls were pock-marked, he saw, when he went up closer. He put his fingers in the holes. Bullet holes. He knew the Republicans had attacked churches, seeing the priests as their enemies, friends of Franco. *Bad things happened on both sides*, Jean-Luc had said.

Nick turned into the street. His contact lived at number four. The houses here were also terraced, and one-storeyed. A light showed through a gap in the shutters at number four. He went up to the door and rapped on it, giving three short knocks and two longer ones. He stood back. Would anyone come? To the left of the door he saw the window shutter twitch slightly and an eye peer out, but only for a second, before withdrawing. He shivered, feeling the cool breeze that had sprung up, replacing the heat of the day.

And then the door opened. Confronting him was a heavily built woman, of around middle-age, with a black apron tied about her middle. He took a step back. She was not eyeing him in a friendly way. Her eyes narrowed as she surveyed him.

'Well?'

'I'm looking for Ricardo,' Nick said nervously.

'*Ricardo?*'

'Does he live here?'

'Eduardo,' the woman called over her shoulder. 'Someone is looking for Ricardo!' She said it as if it were a joke.

Nick's instincts told him that something was seriously wrong. Without waiting for Eduardo to appear he fled, back up to the Calle Real. As he reached it someone stepped out from the shadows and put a hand on his arm.

'You were looking for Ricardo? Come with me. Quickly!'

It was the elderly man with the small dog. He stepped briskly out in front of Nick, who followed, not knowing what else he could do. The man stopped at a house further along the street, opened the door, swiftly ushered Nick inside, and immediately threw the bolt. They were in a narrow unlit hall. The man stood motionless, listening. They heard shouting, and then footsteps went by the door, but none stopped.

When it was quiet Nick's host touched his sleeve and indicated that he should go with him. They went to the back of the house and into a kitchen. There, the man lit an oil-lamp and closed the shutters. They were in a sparsely furnished, stone-flagged room with a wide chimney. Burnt-out logs lay in the grate. Nick could now see his rescuer properly for the first time. He had a face a bit like a walnut, stained brown and criss-crossed with wrinkles. It was the face of a man who had spent most of his life out of doors.

'Are you Ricardo?' asked Nick.

The man shook his head. 'How do you know of him?'

'Francisco the pig man gave me his address. Do you know where I can find him? Ricardo?'

'He lies in a field outside the village.'

'A field?'

'Yes, Ricardo is dead, I'm afraid. Executed, along there by the bridge.'

'*No!*' Francisco had said that Ricardo was a kind man with a great sense of humour.

'His body was allowed to topple over into the stream and lie in the water for two days before another friend and myself took it away in the middle of the night and buried it.'

'But that is terrible!'

'Much is terrible in my country.'

'So, who are the people in Ricardo's house?'

'The man is the leader of the Nationalists in the village. He fired the shot that killed Ricardo so he claimed his house. It was better than his own. The Nationalists are still greedy for blood. They are not content to have won the war, they want revenge. They roam about in gangs looking for Republican sympathisers.'

Nick's knees felt weak and he had to sit down. Moving through this country was like picking one's way through a minefield and each story he heard was more horrific than the last.

'And who are you?' the man asked.

'My name is Nicolás Torres. I am the son of Sebastián Torres.'

The man's eyes flickered.

'Do you know him?'

'No, but I have heard of him, through my friend Ricardo. He came from Scotland to fight for us, didn't he?'

'Yes, he did. So Ricardo was your friend?'

'We were part of the same network of contacts.'

'You helped people?'

'Yes.'

'I need help.'

'Then tell me what I can do for you. My name is Vicente and I give you my word that you can trust me.' The man

17

looked Nick straight in the eye and held out his hand. Nick took it.

He told Vicente his story, saying finally, 'So you see, I need papers.'

'You do, indeed, need them. The guards are stopping people regularly. But I'm sorry, Nicolás, I can't help you with that. I wish I could, but I have no idea how to forge papers!' Vicente threw up his hands. 'Ricardo was the man for that. I can give you shelter for the night and some food and drink – what I have, at least.'

He brought out a heel of bread, a small piece of cheese, an onion and some large plump tomatoes. 'I have a little allotment. It keeps me from starving. We're fortunate, we can grow vegetables. And my goat out the back gives me milk. It's bad in the towns, I hear. Nearly everything is rationed. People are starving. They can buy on the black market, if they have the money.'

While they were eating Vicente noticed the blood-stained rag round Nick's hand and insisted afterwards on taking a look at it. He frowned, not liking what he saw. 'It looks like it's going septic. A barbed-wire wound is not good, especially with animals around.'

He fetched a pail of water from the yard and poured some into a tin basin. There was no running water in the village. They drew what they needed for washing from two wells on the outskirts and their drinking water came from the fountain.

Vicente cleansed the wound as best he could with a sliver of soap, after which he dabbed it with white spirit while Nick held the wrist fast with his other hand in an effort to reduce the pain. Soap, too, was scarce, said Vicente, and because of that diseases were spreading. Men returning wounded from the battlefield were bringing germs back with them. Vicente had just finished when there came a knocking at the front door.

'Quickly,' he said to Nick, 'you must go into the stable.'

He opened the back door and propelled Nick towards a broken-down shed across the yard. 'You'll find some straw there. Hide in that.'

An overpowering stench hit Nick as he opened the stable door. In the dim light he made out a donkey and a goat. He remembered the smell of goat from villages visited with his father when he was younger, before the war. The donkey looked at him but appeared not to be perturbed by this sudden intrusion and the goat paid him no attention at all. In the corner lay a heap of straw. Nick dived into it, pulling the prickly strands on top of himself.

Not long afterwards he heard the back door opening and Vicente's voice saying, 'I tell you, I have seen no stranger in the village tonight.'

'You were out, though, earlier, with your dog, weren't you? Two girls on the bridge saw you. They saw this man too, quite clearly. Tall, carrying a knapsack and a bedroll. My wife confirms all that. She says he was quite young. He was looking for Ricardo.' The last sentence was loaded with meaning.

'He must have passed along the street before me,' said Vicente.

Nick burrowed deeper into the straw. His heart felt as if it were turning somersaults inside his chest. What if they found him and arrested Vicente and took him to the bridge and shot him?

'We'll just a take a look, anyway.'

Boots scraped in the yard. The door of the stable was tugged open and the beam of a torch stabbed the darkness. The donkey brayed and pawed the ground.

'There are only the animals here, as you can see,' said Vicente.

'He's somewhere, this young man, that is certain. He has not vanished up into the sky.'

'He may have left the village by now.'

The light swept from side to side, and was then withdrawn. The men went back into the house. It was quiet again in the stable, except for the sound of an animal chewing.

Nick stayed in his hiding place until Vicente returned to report that the coast was clear.

'I must go, Vicente, or I'll get you into trouble.'

'You need sleep. Stay for the night. You can leave in the early morning before the village is awake.'

'If you're sure?'

'Yes. I will give you the address of someone else further south you can call on for help. You have your bedroll? You'll have to sleep here, though, I'm afraid, Nicolás, with the animals for company. In case they come back.'

Nick unrolled his blanket and settled down in the straw, thinking he would never sleep in this stuffy, stinking shed with the animals shuffling around him. But he did. He was learning, among so many other things, to sleep anywhere.

Four

Vicente woke Nick before it was light. 'Better to get on your way before the sun is up.'

Nick washed in the yard from the tin basin. When he had rinsed his face with cold water he felt himself coming to life again. He had been deep in sleep when Vicente shook his shoulder. Even after washing he could smell the animals on his hands and arms. It was a pungent smell that would linger for a long time.

On the kitchen table Vicente had set out a bowl of goat's milk, a piece of bread and a thin slice of cheese. Nick did not feel hungry but ate since he would need as much energy as he could muster for the next leg of the journey. He had a vision of the map of Spain in his head. It was a huge country, several times bigger than Scotland. He had estimated that he would have to cover well over a thousand kilometres if he were to go as far as the Andalusian coast where his grandparents lived. Or, perhaps, used to live. Since the war had started he had not known if they were alive or dead. There had been no word from them.

'Let me see your hand,' said Vicente. Nick held it out, palm up. Vicente made a face. 'Doesn't look too good to me. Try not to get more dirt in it. Perhaps Julio will be able to get you some antiseptic.'

Julio was the next name on Nick's list. He had been mentioned, too, by Francisco, and by Jean-Luc.

'Julio always manages to get money.' Vicente grinned. 'I am sure he will know how to get papers. He is known as "The Fixer".'

The thought cheered Nick. A fixer was what he needed. If he had papers he might at least have a chance to get past the guards, should they stop him, though the very idea of being questioned by them was terrifying.

After he'd eaten, he shook his blanket free and rolled it up. Vicente filled his water-bottle and insisted on giving him some bread and cheese to take with him. Nick thanked him and hoisted his knapsack and bedroll on to his back.

'*Buena suerte*, Nicolás! said Vicente. Good luck.

Nick walked quietly along the Calle Real, resisting the desire to break into a run and put the village behind him as fast as he could. Not every house would hold a potential enemy but the trouble was not knowing who would be for him and who against him. Vicente had said the village had been fairly evenly divided during the war, but now the Nationalists dominated. Nothing was moving in the street, except for the steady trickle of water down the middle. The shutters were all closed up tight; the villagers appeared still to be in their beds and sleeping.

And then a shutter was thrown with a whack, back against the wall, two doors along. The sudden noise startled Nick. Someone was up! With a noise like that he imagined half the village would now be awake. He shrank back into a doorway and waited for a moment, but hearing no other sound he ducked low, and keeping his head beneath window level, passed the house without anyone shouting after him. He broke into a jog. He was nearing the end of the street, could see the last of the houses coming up. A cock crowed in someone's yard. Close by, a dog barked. The cock crowed again. Then a dog, on the opposite side of the street, began to join in.

Now he was through the village and the road before him was empty. In the east the sky was lightening rapidly.

* * *

He must have been walking for an hour when he heard an engine, but before he could find shelter a van had come around the corner and was pulling up.

'Want a lift, lad?' asked the driver. 'I could take you fifty kilometres or so down the road. I've a delivery to make.'

Nick hesitated. It would be a good lift, the offer was tempting, and his feet ached from yesterday's long walk.

'You were at Vicente's last night, weren't you? I live across the street from him. Don't worry. Any friend of Vicente's is a friend of mine. We sing the same songs.' The man leant across and opened the passenger door. 'Come on, lad, get in!'

'But the Civil Guard – I don't have any papers. I wouldn't want to get you into trouble.'

'They'll not be out on the side-roads I take. Not this early.'

Nick went round to the passenger side. If the man was a friend of Vicente's he must be safe. But *was* he a friend? He still hesitated.

'I think I must smell a bit,' he said.

'Goat. I'm used to the pong. Relax. Toss your stuff in the back and get in.'

Nick preferred to keep his knapsack and bedroll on his knee, in case he'd have to fling open the door and make a run for it. The man wanted to talk.

'Where are you heading?'

'I don't know yet.'

'You don't know?'

'It depends.'

'Where are you from, then? I guess you do know that!'

Nick felt he couldn't say Scotland for that would raise too many other questions. 'Nerja,' he said. It was his grandparents' village and where his father might have gone if he'd managed to escape.

'Nerja? Where's that?'

'It's a small fishing village on the Mediterranean.'

'You're a long way from home, then.'

The man chatted on, telling him about his own family, about his daughter who had married a man from Madrid who, in his opinion, was a good-for-nothing, and his son who was still at school and mad about football, like every other boy in his class.

'You going to be a fisherman yourself?'

'Probably not.'

'It's a poor living for most of them, from what I hear.'

It was why his parents, after they'd married, had left Spain and come to Scotland, where his father had got a job working on an estate in the Highlands as an under-keeper. By the time he'd left to go to the war he'd become head-keeper. He enjoyed being out of doors. He had loved his job but he had lost it now and might never get it back. Also, it was said that there might well be war with Germany and, if so, men of his father's age would probably be conscripted. During the Civil War here in Spain, Germany and Italy had supported Franco; they had sent aeroplanes, weapons and ammunition and given the Nationalists a big advantage.

They were travelling over bumpy, single-track roads, riddled with potholes. Nick began to think that the driver himself had a reason to avoid the Civil Guard. He could be operating on the black market. They rejoined the main road, which was only slightly less pitted, and shortly afterwards, on reaching the outskirts of a town, pulled up.

'I'll let you out here, lad. I'm going on in. I have a bit of business to see to.'

Nick thanked the man, feeling guilty that he'd doubted him in the beginning. He waved and watched until the van disappeared from his sight. He felt lonely when it had gone but cheered up when he calculated that he must have only about ten kilometres or so to go to reach Julio. About six miles.

He skirted the town and was on the open road again. As usual he kept close to the edge so that he could take cover if he heard a vehicle. Only one or two passed. He reached Julio's farm in just over two hours. Normally he should have been able to walk that distance in less, but the sun was hot, his hand hurt, and he was feeling a little dizzy, though he had been doing his best to ignore it.

He saw the house from some distance off, sitting in the middle of a plain, surrounded by a fan of oak trees. It was stone-built, two-storeyed, bigger than the average farmhouse, with three red-roofed outbuildings forming an L shape alongside it. The layout had been described to him in detail. In a large field to the side of the house wheat was growing and in the one at the back a few sheep and goats grazed. Julio looked a more prosperous farmer than most Nick had seen. Of course, he was called 'The Fixer', wasn't he? Nick quickened his step.

The man standing at the edge of the wheat field tallied with Vicente's description. Medium height, balding, heavy eyebrows, broad in the chest, short in the legs. He looked up as Nick approached.

'I'm looking for Julio,' said Nick. He hated this moment of addressing people, having to ask for favours.

'Julio who?'

No surnames had been given to Nick, only nicknames, or names used as codes. He could hardly say Julio the Fixer!

'I don't know. Just that he is a friend of Vicente's and Francisco the pig man.'

The man's face changed then and he said brusquely, 'Never heard of them.'

'Your name is not Julio?' persisted Nick, feeling desperate. He had set a great deal of store on Julio the Fixer, recommended to him by three people in all. 'Jean-Luc the Frenchman said he knew you too.'

'I told you – I don't know any of them.' The man took a step closer to Nick. 'So, what do they call you?'

'Nicolás,' he answered without giving it any thought, adding, 'I'm the son of Sebastián Torres,' hoping that might do the trick. He badly needed help. He needed papers and antiseptic cream and, if possible, a painkiller for his hand.

'Look, boy, I'm busy. And you're trespassing.'

With that, the man turned and went striding off across the field towards the house.

Five

Dejected, Nick returned to the road and sat down on the verge. He suspected that the man was Julio, for he had not denied it, and he felt sure that all the names he had mentioned, including his father's, had meant something to him. But the message the man had transmitted was loud and clear: he did not want to be involved, not any more.

Nick forced himself up on to his feet. As he was passing the house he glanced across and saw a woman's face at the window. She was watching him. And he thought he saw a shadow behind her. He looked away quickly. Perhaps they'd had enough trouble during the war and wanted to be left alone. He could understand that. Why should they put themselves in danger for someone they had never seen before? Or perhaps they'd moved sides to support the Nationalists instead of the defeated Republicans. That was an alarming thought and one that made him hurry along faster. Francisco had said that some people had shifted once they'd seen which way the wind was blowing. It was not uncommon in wars. They wanted to save their skins.

Nick wondered if he were becoming overly suspicious, though the need to be sceptical had been dinned into him. *Don't trust anyone until it has been demonstrated to you that he – or she – is trustworthy*. He realised that he had not been careful enough when talking to Julio. He had blurted out his own name, and his father's name. His father might be on a blacklist, a known Republican.

Feeling even more alarmed, he veered off to the right on a narrow track once he'd passed the farm, cut through a small wood and scrambled to the top of a hillock which would give him a good viewpoint.

Julio was standing at his gate but he was not looking in his direction, he seemed to be watching the traffic. He might be waiting for an expected visitor to arrive. He might be doing anything, but until Nick found out what it was he would wait. *Always wait if you're not sure. Play safe. Hang back.*

A low-slung van with a smoking exhaust went past, followed by a horse and cart, and shortly afterwards came a man on a bicycle, going in the opposite direction. Then Julio stepped out into the road and held up his hand. He was flagging down a car. Nick saw that the driver and the front-seat passenger were wearing the distinctive tricorn hats of the Civil Guard.

He wasted no time. He slid down the bank on the side facing away from the house and broke into a lumbering run, conscious of a lack of energy. His legs felt leaden. When he'd gone a sort distance he flattened himself on the ground behind a thorn bush and listened. Hearing voices, he risked a quick look. The two guards were standing on top of the hillock he had just left and they were scanning the landscape. Nick pulled his head back down and for what seemed like a long time lay watching a line of ants moving in formation across his forearm, up one side and down the other. He felt hypnotised by the tiny insects.

When he did blink and manage to look up, the coast seemed clear, but back on his feet he felt light-headed again. It must be the sun, he decided, though he was wearing the canvas hat that Jean-Luc had made him pack. He had warned him to be careful not to get heat-stroke: *You may not be used to the fierceness of our sun, coming from a cold country in the north.* He wished Jean-Luc was with him now. He might know what to do, which way to go. His injured hand, too, was throbbing. He forced himself yet again to move on.

The terrain was open but hilly and covered with rock and scrub. The stunted trees looked as if they suffered much from the north-east wind. Today there was not even the suggestion of a breeze. The air was absolutely still. He tramped over ground that smelt of rosemary and thyme, reminding him of his mother's garden. The thought of it made him feel homesick for the glen, for the familiarity of it, the security of it. Here, he was sure of nothing, neither the terrain nor what lay ahead. This was not land that could ever be cultivated; at most, it might provide grazing for goats and, indeed, after he had gone a little way, he saw a goatherd with his flock moving across one of the tracks. He lay low until the man and his long thin line of brown beasts had gone over the hill.

Once he had lain down, Nick felt disinclined to move again. He needed a rest, and, more than anything else, liquid to ease his throat. His mouth, his gullet, felt parched. He drank deeply from his water-bottle and could have drunk more but dared not. A little way back he had passed a dried-up river, its bed covered with sludge. He remembered, from earlier visits to Spain in high summer, the dry river beds, in contrast to the fast-flowing spate rivers of his native Inverness-shire, the water amber-coloured from the peaty soil, bubbling over smooth grey stones. How wonderful it would be to plunge, head first, into such a river! At this moment there was nothing he wanted more in the whole wide world.

For a while he lay on his back with his eyes closed against the light trying to hold the picture of such a river, the Spey, in his mind. But he could not do it. The pulsing of his right hand had built up to such a pitch that it was drowning out everything else. He struggled back up on to his feet and gazed around, wondering in which direction he should go. Vaguely south, following the sun, except that it would not be possible to move in a straight line. Spain was too mountainous for that.

Whatever he did he must not allow himself to get lost in among the mountains, the sierras. He knew all about people getting lost in the Scottish Highlands. His father had been part of a mountain-rescue team and had often been called out on searches on wild, snow-filled winter nights. He had never hesitated to go: that was his nature. This was summer, and there would be no snow, and these hills were not as high as the lofty sierras of southern Spain which Nick would come to later, but they were part of a wilderness, covering hundreds, perhaps thousands of square miles. The further he travelled the more he was becoming aware of the immensity of this country. He had no map, no compass, no idea where he was. His head was in a whirl and he felt disorientated.

But it was the torrid, unyielding heat that he was finding so difficult. The maimed trees offered little in the way of shade. He could have heat-stroke, for all he knew. He was conscious that he was walking in an uneven, zigzag way. The sun was climbing higher and higher in the sky. He longed for a breeze, the feel of something cool on his cheeks. He licked his lips. They were rough and bone dry, like the skin of a tortoise he had once had. He unscrewed the cap of his water-bottle, put the mouth of it against his mouth, letting it rest there. Should he drink or not? *Just a little*, he told himself, *not too much. Need to save some for later. Water is scarce. Water is essential. Without water one cannot survive. Don't need to be told that.*

He tipped the bottle, letting a little of the liquid trickle down his throat. How good that felt. He tilted the bottle again. Just a little more, not too much. What a relief it was to feel his thirst slaked even for a moment. Another drop would not matter, surely could not matter. He drank, until the bottle ran dry. And when it did he kept tipping it back, again and again, hoping against hope that there would be another drop to come sliding down into his hot, arid throat.

He staggered when he started to walk again. But he must keep going, he must reach a road and a village or a house and find water. Surely someone would give him a cup of water. He would give anything for a cup of water, anything at all.

He did not see the goatherd until the man was almost upon him.

'Are you all right, lad?'

Nick blinked. The man looked as if he had a double outline. The image was fuzzy and would not stay still.

'Are you all right?' the goatherd asked again.

'Water,' gasped Nick.

'Sit down. Here! Now drink!'

Nick felt the liquid on his lips and opened his mouth to receive it. He gulped and drank and, like a plant after watering, began to revive a little. He opened his eyes and stared into the face of the bearded man.

'Have I drunk all your water?'

'Doesn't matter. There's a spring close by.'

'A spring?' It seemed like a miracle that there could be water at hand.

'I'll show you.'

The goatherd helped him on to his feet and led him through a small copse to some rocks. Out of a crack between two rocks trickled pure clear water. Nick put his mouth underneath and held it there until he started to choke, then he filled his water-bottle until it was brimming over. He grasped the man's hand and spluttered out his thanks.

'You've saved my life.'

'You don't look too good, lad.'

'I'll be fine now, thank you.'

Goat bells were tinkling somewhere. Their keeper had to go and round up his charges. Before he went he said, 'If you want to get out of the sun for a bit, there's a little cave in the rocks just up there.'

It seemed like a second miracle: a hideaway out of the sun. Nick found it and crawled gratefully inside. He was, in fact, feeling absolutely rotten, worse than he could ever remember feeling at any other time in his life. His right hand was on fire and his head was swimming. Shortly afterwards, he lost consciousness.

Six

When Nick came round, he saw, as if through a swirl of mist, a face bending over him. He struggled to sit up, and a hand helped him.

'You're ill,' said a voice.

He blinked and the owner of the voice came into focus. A girl with dark, wide-spaced eyes and long black hair was frowning at him. She wore a black dress unbroken by any colour and he wondered in a vague sort of way if she could be in mourning. Round her neck she wore a small silver crucifix on a thin chain. He wondered, too, if she was real, or merely a mirage.

'I hurt my hand,' he said.

'Let me see.'

He let out a yell when she touched it.

'Sorry! Your hand's in a dreadful state.' She sounded horrified. 'And you look as if you have a fever.'

'I do,' he said weakly.

'I think you've got blood-poisoning.'

He thought so, too, had thought it at intervals, each time he had surfaced from his hallucinations.

'We'll have to get you to the doctor's.'

'Is there one?'

'In the village.'

Could there be a village somewhere in this wilderness? When he was hallucinating he had thought at times that he was on an ice-capped mountain trying to catch his breath; at others, that he was wandering, bare-footed, over a red-hot scorching desert.

'It's about twenty minutes' walk. Do you think you can make it?'

Twenty minutes' walk. So he had not been very far from civilisation all day.

'I'll try.'

'I'll help you.'

Nick took a drink first from his bottle, then braced himself to make the effort. His head swam. The girl put a hand under each of his armpits and more or less hauled him up on to his feet.

'Don't worry,' she said, 'you can lean on me. I'm strong.'

He needed to lean on her, he would have slipped to the ground otherwise. They were in a valley, a fairly flat one with open views and a poplar-fringed river that had virtually dried up. The first part of the going was over stony, untilled ground, where nothing but coarse grass grew, apart from brambles and the odd thorn tree. A small grove of almond trees flourished on a higher slope, and here and there a chestnut or a walnut tree. The girl drew his attention to them, in an effort perhaps to divert him from his pain.

After they'd gone a short distance, she stopped to point out a spire in the distance. 'See that church and those roofs? That's our village. It's not far.'

It was only a blur before Nick's eyes. He had to trust her to take him there.

They dropped height a little and came to a large field where a few beasts grazed, half a dozen cows and sheep, a number of donkeys and one or two mules. After that the land was divided into numerous small allotments. Most villagers had one, she told him, for growing vegetables for the table, not for sale. They took a detour round their perimeter and saw an old man bent double in the middle of his plot.

'Nearly there,' said the girl encouragingly.

The doctor lived at the northern end of the village, in a detached house with a large garden, set apart from the rest, which meant that they did not have to pass any other houses.

The girl opened the black wrought-iron gate, led Nick up the path and rang the bell. The door was opened by a small plump woman in a brown dress and white apron.

'Isabel!' she cried, her eyes transfixed by the sight of Nick.

'Marina, is the doctor at home?'

'He is. Come in!'

Between them, Marina and Isabel helped Nick up the step and into the vestibule.

'What is it, Marina?' asked a voice from further up the hall.

'Doctor, Isabel has brought a young man. He looks in a bad way.'

They took Nick into a small white room and laid him on a bed. What a relief to lie down! He let his eyes close. Overhead a fan whirled madly in an effort to cool the air.

'He's injured his hand,' said Isabel.

Nick felt firm fingers encircle the wrist of his burning hand. He heard disjointed words floating around his head which he could not quite comprehend.

Nasty . . . don't like the look . . . seen lots like this . . . in the war . . . blood-poisoning . . . risk of gangrene . . . have to cauterise . . . Marina, brandy . . . aspirin . . .

Someone held his head and he felt a glass clink against his teeth.

'Drink,' said Marina. 'This will help dull the pain.'

The liquid stung his throat and made him gasp, but he let it trickle away down his throat.

'A bit more,' urged Marina. 'Drink as much as you can. And swallow this little pill.'

He swallowed and drank.

'That should do now, Marina,' said the doctor. 'Fetch some cold wet cloths for his forehead, please. We need to try to lower his temperature. Isabel, do you think you could hold his wrist while I work on his hand?'

'Of course.'

'Good, good. You would make an excellent nurse. Or doctor! I've told you that before, haven't I? Now, grip his wrist as tightly as you can while I work.'

After the first excruciating shaft of pain which seemed to consume his entire being, Nick lost consciousness.

When he surfaced some time later the pain was still there, and no less fierce, though it felt different in a way he could not have defined.

'Are you awake?'

He opened his eyes to see Marina bending over him. The light in the room was grey except in a corner where a small lamp burnt on a table.

'Is it evening?' he asked, his voice emerging as a croak.

'It is. You've been sleeping for some hours.'

Marina helped him to drink some water and swallow another pill, then she lifted a towel and dried his forehead. He realised that his clothes were sticking to his body.

'That's what you need to do, sweat out the fever. That's what will cure you. I'm going to help you put on this nice clean nightshirt and then I'll wash and dry your clothes for you.'

It was an agony to undress and allow the loose white shirt to be eased over his head. Each movement was an effort and he had to bite his lip to stop himself from crying out. Marina supported him, saying, 'Nearly finished. You're doing very well. Good lad, good lad.'

He lay back exhausted and let his eyes roam round the room.

'Isabel has gone home,' said Marina, as if reading his thoughts.

'She lives near by?'

'At the other end of the village.'

He must thank her. She had saved his life. 'She'll come back?'

'I expect so, in the morning. She will want to know how you are doing. But what you must do now is sleep, recover your energy.'

He nodded, closed his eyes again. Marina pulled up a sheet and tucked it under his chin, reminding him of how his mother used to do it when he was small.

'Thank you,' he murmured.

'If you need me, just call out. Don't hesitate. I shall be in the kitchen, next door to here. And Dr Fuentes is across the hall.'

A bell rang somewhere.

'Someone at the door!' exclaimed Marina. 'I wonder who that can be at this hour. Not another patient, I hope. We've had a busy day.'

She left the room, leaving the door to stand ajar, and went to see who the caller was.

Perhaps it's the girl, Isabel, thought Nick. *Maybe she has come back to see me.*

But it was a man who answered Marina's greeting of '*Buenas noches*'. Good evening.

Then the doctor's voice joined in. 'Ah, Roberto, I thought you might be paying us a visit. Isabel has told you about our young man, I suppose?'

'She said she came across him in the *campo* in a state of collapse and brought him to you.' This man had a harsh voice, one that made Nick immediately recoil. This was not a well-wisher.

'She is a kind girl.'

'Perhaps. But I don't like the idea of her befriending strange men, wounded or not. There are too many Reds and bandits about. Anyway, how is he, your patient?'

'It'll be touch and go. He should have a crisis during the night when the fever peaks. We'll have to see if he survives that.'

'I've a feeling he will,' said Marina. 'He's a determined lad, I can sense it. A fighter.'

'Who is he, do you know?'

'He's not been in a fit state to answer questions.'

'No papers?'

'No idea. He was carrying nothing.'

'What about his clothes, Marina? Do you have them?'

'Well, yes. I've just been helping him to undress.'

'Fetch them, please.'

Marina came back into Nick's room. 'Don't worry,' she whispered, then she scooped up his clothes from the floor and went back to rejoin the two men.

'I was just going to wash them,' she said.

'Let's have a look first. Couple of pesetas in that pocket and some cents. Doesn't tell us much. Certainly no sign of papers. What about the other pocket? Now that's interesting. A penknife.'

'How so?' asked Dr Fuentes.

'It's not Spanish. Made in England. Look, do you see, Doctor?'

'I dare say you might be able to buy them here. Before the war, of course. It doesn't look very new.'

'He speaks Spanish,' put in Marina.

'He had no haversack with him? No bag of any kind?'

'Nothing.'

I must have left it in the cave, thought Nick, *with my water-bottle and bedroll. I must get them back before I move on. I shall need them.*

'Odd, isn't it, wouldn't you agree? A complete stranger wandering in the *campo* without any identification or belongings except for an *English* penknife?'

'We've had a lot of strangers wandering about in recent times, have we not?' said Dr Fuentes. 'Men returning home after the war.'

'Yes, your patient might have been trying to do that. The penknife makes me wonder though if he might not have been left behind by one of the International Brigades.'

'He wouldn't have been old enough to fight in the war,' said Marina. 'I'd say he was about sixteen, the same age as your Isabel.'

Your Isabel. Could this man whom he could hear but not see be Isabel's father? Nick found it difficult to connect the two in his head.

'We had some boys of fifteen and sixteen fighting for us. Proud to fight. Let's have a closer look at his clothes.'

Thank goodness Jean-Luc told me to cut out all the labels, thought Nick.

'Well, well. Look at this, Doctor! The label has been cut out from his shirt and his trousers. I wonder why he would have done that? Perhaps to conceal his country of origin? I think I'd like to see this young man.'

'You can see him, Roberto, but you won't be able to question him.'

'He's sleeping,' said Marina. 'I gave him a pill.'

'I am only going to look. I might even recognise him.'

'He's in the surgery,' said Dr Fuentes. 'Through the back.'

Nick lay still, controlling the trembling in his legs as best he could, and kept his eyes shut. This man, whoever he was, whatever he was, spelled danger. They were coming along the hall, pushing back the door of his room and now entering. He was aware of a shadow bending over him.

'I'm fairly sure I haven't seen him before. And I know most of the young men in the villages round about.'

'I expect you do,' said Dr Fuentes, 'in your job.'

His job, thought Nick, *what can his job be? A butcher, a baker, a candlestick maker?* His thoughts were becoming more muddled and hazy by the minute.

'He looks Spanish,' offered Marina.

The man grunted. 'Well, there's obviously nothing to be done for the present. I'll come back tomorrow.'

'He'll need twenty-four hours at the very least,' said Dr Fuentes. 'I would be very unhappy to have a patient disturbed while he's fighting a fever.'

'Very well. Day after tomorrow then, in the morning. How about that? I doubt if he needs to be guarded. He's obviously in no shape to run off anywhere.'

The man laughed, but the other two did not join in. Nick felt the shadow move away from his bed. He opened his eyes to take a quick look. The man was wearing the uniform of the Civil Guard.

Seven

Sleep came over Nick in a relentless wave, sweeping him up and sucking him under. He felt himself going down as if to the bottom of the sea and was happy to go. Oblivion was what he wanted. He slept a deep but troubled sleep, broken by nightmares and spells of raving, during which he was tended by Marina talking to him in a soothing voice and wiping his brow with a cold wet cloth. In the morning she told him that his fever had peaked just after midnight, and from then on he had become calmer.

He felt weak but at least his mind was clear. Marina brought him some warm milk, which comforted his dry throat, and then, at her urging, he forced down a piece of dry bread and a few green olives. She told him he must try to rebuild his strength. He remembered the man in the grey-green uniform, could hear his voice in his ear: *He's obviously in no shape to make a run for it.* He had to get into shape and make a run for it, and he had to do it quickly, before the man came back.

'You were crazed in the night,' said Marina. 'You raved. I could not understand much of what you said.' She glanced round, making sure the door was closed before she added quietly, 'You were speaking English.'

He understood what she meant but, also, that she would not betray him.

'A man came here last night,' he said.

'He is a sergeant in the Civil Guard. He's in charge of the station in the village.'

'And Isabel?'

'She is his daughter.'

So Isabel had betrayed him! Yet he had trusted her. He could have sworn, when he looked her in the face and met her eye, that she was trustworthy. There had been an openness in her look, just as there was in Marina's now. Could he have been mistaken? Could he be sure that Marina would not betray him too?

'She's a fine girl, Isabel. She's had to take over the care of her family. Her mother went to pieces when they lost the eldest boy.'

Nick did not ask how or when the boy had been 'lost'. In the war, he presumed.

'This is mainly a Nationalist village,' said Marina, taking on the quiet, guarded voice again. 'It's staunchly pro-Franco. Not everyone is for him, of course, but those who are not know well enough to keep their mouths shut. We have seen terrible fighting here, reprisals and counter-reprisals. Many of our young men have been shot and killed. Or hanged. Yes, that, too. We want peace now.'

She straightened herself up as the door opened and Dr Fuentes came in.

'Marina, you go and get some sleep. You've been up all night.'

'And you, Doctor, for much of it.'

Nick was alarmed. Had the doctor heard him raving in English too? Was he pro-Franco? He had sounded friendly enough to the sergeant, Isabel's father. But perhaps he had no choice. No one could afford to get on the wrong side of the guards.

'I got some sleep after midnight,' said Dr Fuentes. 'So, off you go, Marina! You need your rest too.'

When she had gone Dr Fuentes took the chair beside the bed that she had vacated.

'I think you are going to make it now, lad. It will take some time for your hand to heal and you'll have to be careful not to get a secondary infection in it. I wouldn't give much for your chances if you did. It will have to be dressed regularly. Where will you be heading for when you leave here?'

Nick had a ready answer prepared and used it now, feeling a little guilty that he was about to lie to the doctor who, as far as he could judge, was a good and an honest man. But then, thinking of Isabel, it seemed that he was not such a good judge of character after all.

'Toledo,' he said.

'Ah, Toledo. I know it quite well.'

Nick's heart did a plummet.

'You have family there?'

'My grandparents.'

'Which part do they live in?'

'In the centre.'

'Near the castle?'

'Quite near.'

'You have some distance still to go, then?'

Nick felt anxious. Why was the doctor asking him so many questions? Would he go straight to the sergeant and tell him what he had found out about him?

'Let's have another look at your hand and see if I can clean it up a bit more.'

Nick needed brandy, again, to cope with the ordeal.

'By the time it's healed we'll have turned you into an alcoholic!'

Nick was in too much pain to smile. After the hand had been rebound he was given a painkiller, by which time he was ready to sleep again. He was in no shape to run anywhere.

Before the doctor left the room he bent over him and said quietly, 'By the way, lad, there is no castle in Toledo. Perhaps your grandparents live near the river. The River Tajo.' And with that, he went out.

Nick's next visitor was Isabel. He was in that state of being half asleep, half awake, when he heard Marina's voice.

'I'll see if he's awake.'

'Don't disturb him if he's not,' said Isabel.

He did not want to see her, could not bear to have to talk and pretend that she was a good friend. So she had saved his life and brought him here, but only to deliver him into the hands of her father afterwards. She must know that strangers wandering in the *campo* would be regarded with suspicion, that they would be questioned by the guards, and that if they did not give the right answers they would not escape lightly. She was her father's daughter, after all. And there could not be a soul living in Spain who did not know about the cruelty and torture that had taken place on both sides of the divide. He closed his eyes.

The door opened and he was aware of Marina approaching the bed, then retreating again.

'He's sound asleep, Isabel.'

'In that case . . .'

'Yes, it's best not to waken him.'

'Tell him I came though, will you?'

'I will. Look in later, dear.'

'I have to go and visit Father's sister, Aunt Arrieta. I won't be back till late. I'll come in the morning.'

Her father, too, had said he would return in the morning, but, in fact, he came later that afternoon. Nick heard Marina talking to him in the hall.

'No, he is not properly conscious yet, Sergeant Morales. It has been a bad fever. It has abated somewhat but he is still very ill indeed. Dr Fuentes left orders that no one was to visit him.'

'Tomorrow morning, then, as agreed. I am not prepared to put it off any longer.'

'*Buenas tardes*, Sergeant.' Good afternoon. Marina said it with a finality that suggested that he should not trouble her again that day. Nick smiled.

She came into the room. 'Could you eat an egg now? I have a lovely fresh one, laid only this morning by the doctor's hen. We only have one hen – the rest were all stolen – but she does her best by us.'

She brought in a tray with the egg lightly boiled, a thick slice of bread dressed with olive oil and a mug of warmed milk, and sat by him until he had finished every last crumb.

'You are picking up, I think?'

He had been out of bed and had managed to walk to the toilet, his legs buckling a bit as he went, that was true, but at least he had made it there and back, unsupported.

'Marina, I can't stay here much longer.'

Her face looked troubled. 'You are not fit to leave.'

'I have to, before tomorrow morning. You know that, don't you?'

'I'm afraid I do. But you must have another good night's sleep first. You can leave before first light. You can't walk in the dark. The sergeant won't come before eight or nine.' She shook her head. 'But where will you go?'

'I know somewhere I can hole up not far away. I'll stay there until I'm fit enough to move on.'

'I'll get you up just before six. I'll make sure that I do, don't worry. We have a bargain then – you promise me to sleep well and I will wake you in good time.'

In the evening, Dr Fuentes dressed Nick's hand again and pronounced himself pleased with his progress. 'Early days yet, of course, very early, but so far we can say so good.'

For supper Marina brought more milk and bread, a couple of juicy tomatoes and some olives.

'I have to eat all this?'

'All!' she declared firmly. 'Or else I won't wake you in the morning.' She looked at him for a moment, then said, 'I don't even know your name. I would like to know it.'

'Nicolás,' he said.

'Nicolás, how old are you? Sixteen?'

Nick nodded.

'You are very young. Many boys your age have lost their lives in our war. Be careful.'

By the time he had eaten the sun had gone down and he was ready for sleep. Without a good night's rest he would make it no further than the garden wall. Marina handed him a painkiller, then she turned out the lamp.

'Sleep well, Nicolás,' she said and left him.

He would have to trust her to wake him. A small doubt still niggled, telling him that it was foolish to trust anyone but yourself. Hadn't Jean-Luc stressed that? And hadn't Isabel betrayed him? So why not Marina? Then he shook himself. He was being unfair doubting her for even a second; she had been so good to him. It was possible to recognise good people.

Civil wars must be the worst wars of all: they made people distrust even their best friends.

Eight

Marina did not let him down. A little before six, she shook him gently by the shoulder. 'Time to get up.' She had laid out his clothes, freshly washed and dried, over the chair at the foot of the bed.

He felt uncertain on his feet when he got out of bed and had to stand still for a moment to get his balance.

'Are you sure you will be all right?' Marina's arms were ready to catch him if he should fall. 'What a silly question! Of course you're not sure. But you are going anyway.'

He went to the toilet along the corridor, taking care to make as little noise as possible so that he would not disturb Dr Fuentes. He had to touch the wall all the way along to keep himself steady. When he returned Marina was laying out food on the bedside table, which she insisted he eat straight away.

'I won't let you go until you do!'

And in a brown paper bag, ready for him to pick up, she had put half a round of bread, a dozen or so black olives, a wedge of cheese, a sausage, and some tomatoes that had the smell of being freshly picked. She must have been out in the garden in the dark. How good she was. And how stupid he had been to doubt her. He felt ashamed now.

In addition, she had packed a roll of new bandages, a packet of lint, some plasters and a tube of antiseptic cream.

'Whatever else you do, you have to keep that wound clean, remember! And these pills will help if you get any pain.' She gave him some round pills, which he put in a trouser pocket.

'I will always remember you, Marina. You have saved my life.' Along with Isabel. But he tucked that particular thought away into the back of his mind.

'I've done nothing much. But I'd like to know you're all right once you get to your destination.' She had never asked him where he was going.

'I'll try to send word. A letter. I won't sign it, but you'll know.'

'You must do that.'

She embraced him and he held on to her, wishing he did not have to leave, not yet. If only he could have waited until he felt a bit stronger. Could he make it as far as the cave? He was about to find out.

A bird was beginning to send up an occasional chirp.

'You had better go,' said Marina. She went ahead of him.

A door opened further along the dark hall. Nick stopped.

'Good luck, lad,' said Dr Fuentes. 'And if your hand gets worse again you must come back.'

'Thank you, Doctor. Thank you for everything.'

Marina opened the front door. The morning air smelt fresh and clean and Nick's spirit lifted. He gave Marina a last hug, went up the path, opened the black, wrought-iron gate, and headed out across the *campo* as dawn was breaking over the fields.

For the first few yards he had a surge of energy and walked with quite a springy step, but after that his stamina dropped sharply. His legs felt so weak he was not sure he would be able to make it as far as the cave. Twenty minutes from there to the village, Isabel had said. He reckoned that would be about a mile and, in his present state, it might take him half an hour.

It took two hours. He had to crawl for the last part of the way, or rather wriggle his way over the ground, since one hand and arm were out of action. His good hand propelled him forwards, as well as dragging along Marina's bag of food. His legs had given up and folded under him, as if they were stuffed with straw. Drops of perspiration dripped from his forehead. At one point he lay still, face down on the earth, wondering if he would ever be able to move again, or whether he would have to lie there, letting the sun overhead bake him until he was nothing but a dried-out husk. Then he rallied and made the last spurt that carried him as far as the cave.

He lay on its soft floor, panting from the exertion, relieved to be out of the sun, then he groped around until he found his water-bottle. It was only partly full so he was careful to drink no more than a few drops, not knowing when next he would be able to go as far as the spring. At the moment, making the smallest journey seemed like scaling the highest peak in the Sierra Nevada mountains near his grandparents.

He would not stay long. To linger could be dangerous since it was here that Isabel had found him. Once it was discovered that he was missing she might tell her father about the cave. Would the sergeant think he was important enough to come after him? He had no idea. He could not be bothered to think. He dozed.

Voices roused him. Men's voices, calling to each other. Nick blinked, wondering where he was, and then, panicking, he struggled up into a sitting position. There was no chance, however, that he could make a run for it.

The men were right outside the cave and there seemed to be three of them, as far as he could make out. He strained to hear what they were talking about. A horse, was that it? At least it did not appear to be him! They were having an argument. He gathered that there was only one horse and three men but he could not understand why they did not know to whom the horse belonged. The voices were becoming more and more heated and more and more aggressive and then came the sound of scuffling and swearing. Finally, one of them let out a scream that sent a shiver up Nick's spine.

After that there was silence until it was broken by one voice saying, 'Idiot! Fool! *Vamos*!' Let's go!

They went. Nick listened to the trample of the horse's hoofs until they faded and all was quiet around him again. What about the man who had let out the bloodcurdling yell? Was he moaning? Or was it the wind sighing? Nick did not go out to look. He stayed where he was, apprehensive, wondering what next would happen.

Some time afterwards, the Civil Guard arrived, two of them. Nick thought he recognised the voice of Isabel's father. They were not looking for him though. It was the man who had screamed who was interesting them.

'That's one of them all right.'

'Looks like he's been stabbed. Yes, he has. And see, there's the knife.'

'Any sign of life?'

'No. He's a goner.'

'OK, we'll have to get a donkey to bring him over to the station.'

And that was that. Life was cheap here. Nick had learnt that since crossing into Spain.

The guards moved away.

He was trapped now in his cave, unable to move while the dead man lay outside awaiting a donkey to carry him away. It seemed a long time before anyone returned. Nick fancied he heard the drone of flies.

The two men who eventually arrived were not guards. They might be the owners of the donkey. They were obviously not pleased at being sent out on this job and had a few words to say about the sergeant that were not complimentary. Then they sat on the ground and smoked cigarettes. Nick began to wonder if they would stay there all day.

The cigarettes finished, they had a struggle to raise the dead man and lift him on to the animal. After a lot of shouting and cursing on their part and braying and stampeding on the donkey's, they appeared to manage it.

'*Vamos!*'

Nick let out a sigh of relief once they had finally gone. He realised then that he was hungry; it had been a long time since breakfast. He opened Marina's bag and took out the tomatoes. They were bashed and split from being dragged along the ground but they tasted good. He tore off a hunk of bread and ate it with a couple of olives and a piece of the spicy sausage ending with a swig of water. Food had taken on a different meaning since he'd arrived in Spain. Each mouthful was something to be grateful for, especially when he knew that some people were starving. Later on, he would go to the spring to refill his water-bottle. He would stay in the cave overnight. After all, he reasoned, the guards had been right outside and not looked for him, so it seemed unlikely they would return.

In the early evening, when it was cooler, he ventured out. It felt good to be in the open air again and able to stand upright. He stretched himself. Surveying the horizon, he saw no sign of any other human being, only the pale blurs of sheep in the distance. He felt stronger and his hand was less painful. His mind was more at peace, too. Perhaps his luck had turned.

He stayed a while at the spring, drinking from it, filling his water-bottle, holding his good hand in the water, enjoying the coolness. He watched as the sun began to sink, flooding the fields with gold. Feeling refreshed, he began to walk back towards the cave.

He stopped before reaching it. Standing in front of the entrance was Isabel.

Nine

'How are you?' Isabel asked. 'How is your hand?'

'Better,' Nick said gruffly, glancing away from her.

'Are you going to sleep here tonight? In the cave?'

'Why do you ask?' Now he did look her in the face. 'So that you can run back and inform your father?'

'Is that what you think?'

'What else? You did, didn't you? Leave me at the doctor's and run on home to tell your father?'

She shook her head. 'It wasn't like that. Can we go into the cave? I don't think we should stand out here in the open.'

'Are you alone?'

'Of course! Look for yourself if you want to!'

Nick hesitated. *Everyone is an enemy until proved otherwise*. Yet another of Jean-Luc's cautionary warnings. He scrambled up a small knoll which would give him a vantage point. It was not much of a climb but it taxed his strength and he had to rest at the top to let his heartbeat slow down. From here he could look across the *campo* almost as far as the village.

There was not a soul to be seen, unless somebody was hiding in the copse of almond trees, tinged pink in the evening sun. Nothing seemed to be moving, not even the wind. He slid back down the hillock, stumbling as he reached the bottom and feeling a little ashamed. Doubting Thomas! He avoided Isabel's eye again.

She put out a hand to steady him. 'You're not well yet, are you? You should be resting. Come on, let's go into the 'cave.' She led him inside and helped him to sit down. Then she sat herself.

'Sorry I haven't got any chairs,' Nick said.

Isabel might have smiled but the light in the cave was too dim for him to see the expression on her face. He could just discern her outline. She had her knees bunched up to her chin, with her arms encircling them.

'My young brother saw us coming into the village,' she said. 'He saw me taking you into Dr Fuentes' house. *He* told my father.'

'I'm sorry, I shouldn't have blamed you.'

'I don't think Pedro intended any harm. He probably saw no reason not to mention it.'

'Why have you come?'

'I was worried when I heard you'd gone. I knew you couldn't have recovered that easily.'

There had been a rumpus in the village, she told him, when his absence was discovered. Dr Fuentes and Marina were claiming to know nothing about it. 'They said you must have gone in the night while they were asleep.'

'But they didn't come out looking for me? The guards?' Nick did not want to say 'your father'.

'They were too busy looking for bandits.'

'Bandits?'

'Three of them. They hit a farmer over the head with an iron pipe and made off with his horse.'

'And the farmer?'

'He's in hospital, unconscious. And one of the bandits was found somewhere out in the *campo*, dead.'

'Stabbed,' said Nick, going on to tell Isabel how the bandits had quarrelled over the horse. 'Just outside here. I heard every word.'

She shrugged. Such happenings were not uncommon since the end of the war.

'And the other two men?'

'Father is too busy to go chasing after them. They'll be off his territory by this time.'

Nick was glad to think of them being far away. There would be little chance of their returning to the scene of their crime.

'Why did you leave the doctor's house?' asked Isabel. 'Is it because you don't have any papers?'

'Perhaps.'

Was she going to ask him why he had none and where he was from, and what he was doing wandering around the countryside? How could he tell her that he was looking for his father, who had fought on the opposite side to her father? If he did, she might turn against him. Her allegiance must lie with her family.

He heard her sigh and shift her position a little. It was dark now in the cave.

'I can't tell you why,' he said.

'Were you fighting in the war?' she asked in a low voice.

'No.'

'I'm glad. If you'd fought on the Republican side, it would be difficult for me to be friends with you. My older brother, Juan, was killed by the Republicans.'

It was Nick's turn to be silent. Her father would certainly not show mercy to any wandering Republican sympathisers who crossed his path.

'He was killed at the battle of Teruel. He was eighteen.'

Teruel! The name rang a bell. His father had fought there, too, with Francisco, though Nick knew it unlikely that it would have been his father who had killed Isabel's brother. Thousands of men had fought at Teruel. Thousands had died there. Perhaps his own father among them.

'Juan didn't want to fight. It was not in his nature. He was a gentle boy, he loved working with animals. He would have liked to have been a vet if my parents could have got the money together for him to go to college. My father made him go to the war. He told him it was his duty.'

'I'm sorry,' said Nick.

'I hate war!' Isabel exclaimed violently.

'So do I!'

'So many people have died.'

Suddenly she was weeping, her head bowed in her hands. Nick thought of his father who, for all he knew, might also be dead, and he could not hold back his own tears. He reached out in the dark and put his arms round this girl whom he barely knew and she allowed her face to rest against his shoulder.

After a little while they were quiet, drained of emotion. He rocked her a little. How could he have ever doubted her? She had taken risks for him, was taking one even now by being here in this cave with him. He trembled to think what might happen to her if her father should find them.

'Won't your father be wondering where you are?' he asked.

She lifted her head and dried her eyes on the back of her hand. 'Yes, I'll have to go.'

'What will you tell him?'

'That I went for a walk.'

'In the dark?'

'It was still light when I set out.'

When they emerged from the cave they saw that there was an almost full moon. To Nick the *campo* looked eerie and fraught with concealed dangers in the cool white light. But this, of course, was known territory to Isabel. He warned her, however, to be careful. The two bandits with the horse might have got away but others could be lurking. He wished he could walk with her as far as the outskirts of the village but he would not have the strength. If he were to try he would probably collapse before they got there and then he would be a burden to her. He had burdened her enough as it was. Would he see her again? Could he expect to see her? Could he expect her to put herself in more danger for him?

'I don't even know your name,' she said.

'Nicolás. Though mostly I am called Nick.'

'Nick,' she said, trying it out. 'You know I am Isabel?'

He nodded.

'You must take care of yourself, too, and get plenty of rest. Don't try to do too much.'

'I'll have to move on sometime.'

'Not yet, though. You wouldn't get far.'

He knew that himself and hated this feeling of weakness in his body. He had seldom had a day's illness in his life and had prided himself on his fitness.

'I'll try to come tomorrow, though I can't promise. If I were you I'd try to conceal the mouth of your cave with some branches. And thyme makes a sweet-smelling bed.'

And then she was gone, moving sure-footed and silently over the uneven ground. He stood until his eyes were strained with the effort of peering into the distance, then he went to look for a dead tree and some thyme.

After he had camouflaged the entrance of the cave as best he could, Nick settled down on his bed of thyme. Isabel was right: it did smell sweet. Although he was tired sleep was slow in coming to him that night. He lay in the darkness, kept awake by the fever which still pervaded his body and also by a confusion of thoughts and emotions.

Ten

Nick awoke to the sound of a church bell tolling. Was it Sunday? The days of the week had ceased to have any meaning for him. He felt disorientated in time and place. He had no idea where he was in Spain, other than north of Madrid somewhere. He had no idea what the village was called whose church bell was calling its people to Mass. Among them might be Isabel. And her father.

His hand was throbbing more than it had yesterday. He ought to try to take off the blood-stained bandage, clean the wound and put on a new dressing. But first, he would have breakfast.

He ate his bread and cheese sitting outside in the sun. There was not a cloud to be seen in the great blue expanse of sky. The heat was welcome at this time of day; he had wakened feeling chilly. Later, he would have to keep to his shelter. He drank water from the spring and washed his face and head. Then he went up to the top of the knoll to spy out the land, his legs feeling infuriatingly weak still.

There appeared to be no one working in the fields. The villagers would be in church. Under this regime of Franco's everyone was expected to attend, and if they did not their absence was noted, so Francisco had told him. *Remember, on a Sunday you will be more conspicuous outside a church than inside.* He had many things to remember since it had been out of the question to write anything down. Would he be able to recall all the names and addresses he had been given and might need on his journey? It seemed a tall order. His head felt befuddled. The fever still had a partial grip on him.

The outline of the village wavered in the heat. He wished he had binoculars. He might then be able to see Isabel walking down the street, her head held high. He had noticed that she walked with a straight back. A hawk passed overhead, flying low. He watched as it suddenly plummeted earthwards and with deadly precision scooped up an animal – a small rabbit, by the looks of it. There had been a brief squawk when its neck had been seized by the vice-like talons. Then up into the bright air went the bird again, its soft prey dangling from its sharp beak.

Nick did not stay long on his perch, aware that he himself would be visible to anyone looking in his direction. He felt as vulnerable as the rabbit in the grass had been.

Back inside the cave he took out the box of dressings given to him by Marina. Every action took an effort and made him sweat and when he began to unwrap the old dressing on his hand he found it had stuck to the wound. He tried to ease it off gently, bit by bit. The pain was searing and seemed to be travelling right up his arm. He gasped, bit his lip hard, tasted blood. Another little tug, and his head swam, and after that he gave up.

He reached out for his water-bottle and drank the last remaining drops. He must refill it. Not now, though. Definitely not now. He would not be capable of getting up. He turned his eyes away from the sight of his festering right hand. *Blood-poisoning*, he thought. *Gangrene. Some of the veterans had lost legs through gangrene.*

He wished Isabel would come. She would try to, she had said, but she had not promised. It could be difficult for her to escape, especially on a Sunday when all the family might be at home. Even her father, the sergeant, might have hung up his tricorn hat for the day.

The hours passed slowly. Nick dozed. Waking each time he reached for the water-bottle, forgetting it was empty, eventually throwing it across the cave in disgust. His mouth was too dry for him to eat the stale bread and he had finished the tomatoes.

He dragged himself over to the entrance of the cave and looked out. The sun had moved round to the west. She would not come now. But just as he was abandoning hope, he saw the dark outline of someone approaching. Could it be Isabel? What if it were not? He would be neither strong enough nor quick enough to duck back inside his shelter.

Isabel came into focus.

'I'm sorry I couldn't come earlier—' she started to say, before breaking off to cry out, 'What have you been doing?' She was staring at his hand.

'I tried to dress it but I didn't feel so good.'

'You can't expect to. You will still have the poison in your system. You can expect to have fevers for a while. I'm sorry I haven't got any brandy to give you.' She took over. She helped him back into the cave, then she went out to wash her hands in the spring, using a small piece of precious soap she had brought with her for the purpose.

She worked gently on his hand, removing the remaining pieces of the foul-smelling dressing, cleaning the wound, dabbing it with the antiseptic cream, which made him bite his lip, and, finally, rebinding it. Nick fell into a half-swoon much of the time but Isabel carried on, concentrating on the task. When she had finished she went back out to wash her hands again and to fill up his water-bottle. She held it to his mouth while he drank.

'You're a marvellous nurse,' he said.

'I got plenty of experience during the war. I helped Dr Fuentes when the wounded were brought in. They're still coming, on their way back from the battle fronts. Spain's a big country. It takes a long time to walk from one place to another, especially when you're wounded. You know that yourself.'

Isabel had brought him food. Green grapes, slightly tart, ripe tomatoes, and a piece of flat bread baked by herself that morning.

'Eat,' she said.

Nick ate. It was a relief to have someone to tell him what to do. All day he had felt that his head would not allow him to decide anything. The bread was soft and the fruit moist. He had never tasted a meal as delicious as this one. When he told her so, Isabel smiled.

She settled back against the wall near the entrance. A ray of sun was touching her face, highlighting a blotch high up on her right cheek-bone. He frowned.

'Is that a bruise?'

She touched it. 'It's nothing.'

'It is, isn't it? You didn't have it yesterday.' He thought of the sergeant and his harsh voice. 'How did you get it?'

'Truly, it doesn't matter.'

'But it does! Was it your father?'

She shrugged.

'Was it because you came home late?' Nick knew that Spanish parents were stricter with their daughters than Scottish ones. His cousin Flora, who lived in Glasgow and was about his age, was allowed to go to the pictures with her boyfriend, as long as she came home by ten. No girl from a decent Spanish family would be permitted to do that.

'It's not troubling me, really it's not.'

'He's done it before?'

'Maybe. But don't fuss. It'll fade.'

'Where did he think you were?'

'He thought I'd been seeing a boy. But I didn't tell him that I had! If he sees me speaking to a boy in the street he goes mad. He's hot-tempered, that's all.'

That's all! To Nick, it sounded far too much. He said, 'You mustn't stay late tonight!'

'I won't. But you must tell me something about yourself now! You know quite a lot about me but I know nothing about you.'

'What do you want to know?' he asked apprehensively.

'You're not Spanish, Nicolás, are you? I mean, you speak very well, but not—'

'Perfectly?'

'It's only now and then, when I listen carefully, that I can detect an accent. Most people wouldn't.'

'You're right.'

'I'm not going to tell my father, I think you know that now?'

'I do.'

'Are you Italian?'

It might be logical for her to think so since the Italians in their support of Franco had sent troops as well as arms and aeroplanes. Italy, under the leadership of Mussolini, was a Fascist state at present, like Germany.

'No, I'm Scottish. Half, at least. The other half's Spanish.'

'You've come from Scotland? It's a long way.'

'Quite long.' How much could he tell her? He could hear Jean-Luc's voice inside his head again:

Caution, always exercise caution, even when you think you can trust someone. The less people know about you the less they can reveal, and sometimes people are made to reveal things they do not wish to. There are ways in which they can be made to talk.

'Which half is Spanish?' asked Isabel. 'Your mother or your father?'

'My father.'

'You've come looking for something, haven't you? It's

all right, I won't ask you any more.' She was astute, she had possibly guessed, but she was not going to ask him to confirm her suspicion.

She left, saying she would try to come again and this time he felt confident that she would, as long as her father did not prevent her.

Eleven

Isabel came next day, in the morning, bringing food and a can of milk. They had a cow, one of their most valuable possessions, she said.

She seated herself on a fallen log. She was wearing her long black cotton dress, as usual, with the crucifix at her throat, and leather-thonged sandals on her bare brown feet. Normally Nick would not register very much what a girl was wearing, not every detail, but he was noticing everything about Isabel. He saw how she flicked her hair back over her shoulder when she talked and how white her teeth were when she smiled. Everything about her was neat, and strong. Even to have her near him made him feel stronger.

'Why do you always wear black?' he asked.

'For my brother. My father insists. He says we must never forget Juan. As if I would! I don't have to wear black to remember him. Juan would not have wanted me to.'

'You must miss him?'

'He was my best friend. We were very close. Do you have any brothers or sisters?'

'I'm an only child.'

'And your mother? What is she like?'

'She's got a great sense of humour. She looks on the bright side, on the whole.' Though recently she had not been doing that so much. 'She teaches French and Spanish. That's how she met my father, when she came to Málaga to study.'

'What age was she then?'

'Seventeen.'

'And your father?'

'Twenty-five.'

Isabel was interested in the story of his parents. Nick told her that his father had been working on a farm near Málaga. 'His parents were poor. He'd had to leave school early and find work.'

'That's common. So how exactly did they meet, your mother and father?'

'During Semana Santa.' Holy Week. In those days the Easter celebrations had been spectacular in Málaga, with colourful processions thronging the streets every day. Nick supposed they would have stopped during the war but perhaps they would start up again.

Isabel was still bent on her questioning. 'Your mother's parents? Did they approve?'

'Not really.'

'They thought he wasn't good enough for her?'

'Probably.'

'But they went ahead and married?'

'Not until she had finished her degree and was twenty-one. Her parents wouldn't give their permission before.'

'Did they come round?'

'In the end. My father charmed them.'

'He is a man with much charm?'

'I would say so.'

'It's been a happy marriage for your mother and father?'

Nick had never thought about it before, but he answered 'Yes' now without hesitating. His parents were devoted to each other. He did not mind Isabel's curiosity but he hoped she would not ask any more questions. He changed the subject abruptly, asking if she had managed to get away without being seen.

'I told my mother I was going to the allotment, which I was. Father was called out early, he said he'd be away all day. And Pedro is at school. He doesn't care for it much and often doesn't go, but today he did. He's thirteen, and restless. He talks about the war, says he wished he had been old enough to fight. He can be stupid!'

Now that Nick had finished eating, Isabel changed his dressing and this time he managed to stay conscious.

'It's better than last night.' She nodded with approval. 'I was worried about it. But I think we might be winning.'

The 'we' cheered him. She was not going to abandon him, she would come again, and she did, for a short while in the late afternoon, just to check on him, she said.

The following day, she came again, twice, and the next. He awaited her visits eagerly, watched for her coming. She tended to come around the same time. She brought food and changed his dressings. His hand was beginning to heal and his strength to build, though he could still not walk far and at night the sweats came back. She also brought him something to read. A copy of *The Adventures of Don Quixote*, in Spanish. 'You can read Spanish?'

'Yes. More slowly though than English.'

'This is a shortened version for children. I had it at school. We can talk about it when you've read it.'

They talked a great deal when they were together, about their schools and their different ways of living. Isabel's education was over as far as her parents were concerned but Nick, when he returned to Scotland, would go back to school and then, he hoped, to university. He wanted to study marine biology. He felt fortunate compared to Isabel. He had choices ahead of him. She had few. She had told him that her father had already picked out the man he wanted her to marry. The son of the mayor. She hated him, the mayor's son. She said he was brutish, but his family had a position in the village and her father liked that.

'You can't marry him!' protested Nick.

'My father will make me.'

There are ways of making people talk, ways of making them do what they do not want to do.

Nick said no more.

The days slipped past and he felt in no hurry to leave, though he knew he would have to go soon. It could be dangerous to stay too long on the sergeant's territory.

He was sitting outside reading *Don Quixote* one afternoon when Isabel arrived.

'You're enjoying it?' He admitted that he was and she said, 'You are a bit like a knight-errant yourself.'

That amused him. 'I'm not a knight.'

'Neither was Don Quixote. He just thought he was.'

'I'd need a horse, though. But now the "errant" part, maybe I could qualify for that.'

They were laughing when they became aware that they were being watched. Isabel turned her head sharply.

'Pedro!' she cried, jumping up.

Pedro was a gangly youth, as tall as his sister. He stood beside the thorn tree which had been partially concealing him and stared openly at Nick.

'What's he doing here?' he asked.

'Come with me, Pedro,' said Isabel. 'I want to talk to you.' She took his arm.

He went reluctantly, giving Nick a backwards look over his shoulder. They moved out of sight and earshot. Nick was perturbed. Would he have to make a run for it now that his cover was blown? Leave Isabel to the mercy of her father? They had been careless. *A moment's carelessness can cost you your life.*

He waited at the entrance of the cave. His hand was much better and the pain almost gone. He was fit enough to move on; he'd known that for a while. But he did not want to go, not just yet! He was aware that he did not want to have to say goodbye to Isabel.

After a few minutes she came back. Her expression was serious, though she said, 'Don't worry. It'll be all right.'

'Will he tell?'

'I don't think so. I don't think he'd get me into trouble. I've always helped him when he was in trouble, helped to shield him from Father.'

'But you can't be sure? Isabel, I don't want to get you into trouble.'

'I've also bribed him,' she said ruefully. 'It may not be a very admirable thing to do but with Pedro it works.'

'What have you offered him?'

She shook her head.

'Tell me!'

'My savings.'

'Your *savings*? I can't let you do that. I *won't* let you!'

'It's only money. Pedro likes money.'

'But what were you going to do with it?'

'Nothing much.'

He did not believe her. Perhaps she'd been saving up so that she could escape from the village and not have to marry the mayor's brutish son. Perhaps she'd planned to use it to try to go to college. She would love to be a doctor but that would be too difficult, she'd said. She was a girl and her family would not pay for her to study even if they could. She'd be happy if she could find a way to train as a nurse.

He couldn't let her make that sacrifice for him. 'No!' he cried.

'Truly, Nick, I don't mind. I've already made Pedro the offer. I can't take it back. If I did he would go straight to Father. And then I would be in trouble too.'

'We should have taken more care,' Nick said sadly. He should have taken more care. He had been happy during these sunny days here with Isabel, but he had put her in danger. When they were talking together they had forgotten that the rest of the world existed.

'I'll have to go, Isabel.'

'Not before morning, anyway. It will be dark in a little while and you would have no idea which direction you were going in. Pedro won't do anything before he gets his money. So let me think about it tonight. I'll try to think of somewhere you could be safe for a bit.'

He was about to tell her that he had some addresses of 'safe houses' in his head but he thought, *Better not*. What she'd said was true: he needed another bolt-hole not far away, and then a plan, a route to follow.

She was about to move away when he put a hand on her arm to stop her. 'Isabel,' he said, 'I think I—'

'Yes?'

'I think I may have fallen in love with you.' Nick felt himself blushing. He had never said such a thing to a girl before, like someone in a film.

Isabel smiled. 'Perhaps you only think so because you've been ill and lying here all alone.'

He shook his head. 'No,' he said, and then he kissed her. She did not draw away but when he looked into her face afterwards he saw that she was troubled.

'It's difficult. Too difficult. You know that yourself.' Her voice was quiet. 'I'll have to go now but I'll see you tomorrow morning.'

'You will come?'

'Yes, I will come.'

'You promise?' Was he being selfish asking?

'I promise.'

And so she left him, once again and, as always, he felt the gap left by her absence. He watched her until she was out of sight.

As he turned he thought he heard a movement. He wheeled round quickly but there was nothing to be seen, nothing that would worry him, that was. It must have been an animal. His nerves had been jangled by Pedro's appearance on the scene. Their scene. Isabel's brother had shattered their peace.

He went into the cave.

It must have been no more than an hour later when he did hear something definite, the sound of feet approaching. There was nothing he could do. In the next moment a burly form loomed in the entrance, blotting out the light, and the harsh voice of Isabel's father demanded that he come out with his hands up.

Twelve

Nick came out to find a pistol pointing at his chest.

'Keep them up!' barked the sergeant.

Nick tried to hold his hands steady. His knees were trembling and he didn't know how to stop them. What if they were to give way under him? If he made the slightest movement he might be shot. They might intend to shoot him anyway. Summary executions had been common during the war, and still were. How many times had he been told that? His mind felt numb, so numb that he did not seem to be feeling any emotion at all, not even fear. He had imagined such a moment as this, but now that it had happened it seemed unreal.

There were two of them, the sergeant and a constable. The latter was holding a rifle and had a chain looped round his wrist to which was attached an evil-looking red-eyed dog with long fanged teeth. It was some kind of wolfhound and it liked the look of Nick no more than the men did.

'Lower your hands!'

Nick lowered them.

His wrists were seized and forced behind his back, then clipped roughly into handcuffs.

'Search the cave, Manuel!'

The constable dived into the cave and came back out with Nick's knapsack, bedroll and water-bottle. His survival kit. Manuel had to sling his rifle over a shoulder so that he could carry it all and keep hold of the dog's chain.

'Right, march!' The pistol prodded Nick in the back.

He marched, or rather, stumbled, his way across the *campo*, the pistol urging him forwards every time he tripped. It took all the effort of his will to stay upright. He would not let the men see him humiliated. He could not look at them since they were behind him, but the dog kept in step with him, snarling and snapping at his ankles.

They came into the village at Dr Fuentes' end. Glancing sideways, Nick saw Marina's face at the window as he went by. She might have seen them coming across the fields. She did not wave or give him any signal, but he knew that she felt for him.

The village was bigger than Nick had thought. The narrow potholed main street stretched away ahead, curving out of sight. On either side, houses huddled together, terraced for the most part, their doors opening on to the broken pavement. Everything looked in need of renewal.

They walked up the middle of the street. There was no traffic to get in their way, apart from a man leading a donkey with a load of sticks on its back. When the man saw them he tugged the animal quickly into the side to give them room to go by. They passed a shop, nothing much more than a hole in the wall, from what Nick could see, with its door open. Two women clad in black, who'd been chattering volubly on the step, fell silent at the approach of the Civil Guards with their prisoner. Another woman came out of her house to stare openly. Faces were to be seen at windows. Everywhere there seemed to be eyes, watching. News must have spread quickly. A few men in overalls lounged against walls, smoking. One tossed his smouldering butt right in front of Nick, startling him. He'd never known such a wave of hatred coming from people.

The street, at this point, widened out into a square, with a church on one side. Nick lifted his eyes to look at the familiar spire. It had been a landmark for him, seen from his cave in the *campo*. When he had looked at it he had thought of Isabel.

On the corner of the square four men sat outside a bar, at two round zinc-topped tables, with small glasses of brandy in front of them. They stopped drinking to scrutinise Nick. One spoke.

'Got a Red there, have you, Sergeant?'

'Maybe even a spy.'

'You'll be having some fun then!'

Another drinker muttered something about all that being over. A third said, 'It'll never be over until all the bastards are done for!'

They were back in the narrow part of the street and Nick was urged forwards again. It was getting dark and a few windows showed dim lights. He was on the brink of exhaustion, but if he fell down in the gutter they would doubtless kick him until he got up. He knew enough not to expect mercy in any quarter.

The Civil Guard station was at the extreme end of the village. It was a small, one-storeyed building, attached to a two-storeyed house which looked bigger than most of the ones they had passed. This must be where Isabel lived! There was no sign of anyone at any of the windows.

'Inside!'

Nick was pushed into a dim hall and through to a room at the back. The sergeant lit a lamp on the desk and seated himself behind it. The constable threw Nick's bedroll and water-bottle on the floor, then tipped out the contents of the knapsack.

'Socks, underpants, pullover, shirt, pencil, note pad, nothing written on it, plasters, tube of antiseptic cream. Copy of *Don Quixote*. A reader, eh?'

'Can I see it?' The sergeant held out his hand to take the book. He flipped open the cover and when he saw the name inscribed on the flyleaf he pursed his lips and his eyes narrowed. He then summoned Nick to come and stand at the desk in front of him. Nick wanted to put a hand on the desk to steady himself but did not. The constable remained by the back wall.

The sergeant lit a pungent-smelling cigarette, blew a long stream of smoke into Nick's face, smiled a little smile, and said, 'Now then, my friend with the English clothes, you must tell me who you are.'

'My name is Nicolás MacIntosh,' he said, using his mother's maiden name. He could not go on pretending to be a native Spaniard. He had a story ready, prepared with Jean-Luc. 'I am from Scotland.'

'Scotland eh? Why, then, are you not wearing a skirt?' The sergeant laughed and the constable sniggered.

'We only wear kilts for special occasions.'

'And this is not a special occasion? Tut, tut! So, Scotsman, what are you doing here in our country and how is it you speak Spanish like a native?'

'My mother is a teacher of Spanish.'

'Ah, that is so? She has lived here, then?'

'For a while.' Nick's throat was bone-dry. He swallowed and carried on, 'When she was a student. A long time ago. Twenty years or so.'

'And your father. Does he teach Spanish as well?'

'He is a gamekeeper.'

'In Scotland?'

'Yes.'

'What, then, are you, the son of these two Scottish people, doing wandering about in Spain?'

'I was curious.'

'Curious?'

'I want to be a journalist so I thought if I could write a

piece about General Franco and the new Spain it might give me a chance to get started on a newspaper.'

'A scoop?'

'Well, in a way.'

'Plausible, I suppose.' The sergeant leant forward and said in a soft voice. 'The only thing is I am not convinced.' He smiled and sat back again.

Then he got up, walked slowly round the table and struck Nick across the face with the back of his hand. 'I want the truth now, boy!'

'It is the truth,' spluttered Nick, tasting blood. His lip was split and he thought one of his teeth might have gone.

The sergeant struck him again and putting his face close to Nick's he said, 'That was for daring to lay a hand on my daughter!'

As Nick fell to the floor he felt a heavy boot meet the tail-end of his spine. The pain was acute. He groaned. He had no energy to make any other sound. He lay with his cheek flattened against the cold concrete floor, watching a large hairy black spider scuttle towards the crack under the door.

'Take him into the cell!' The sergeant was almost screaming now.

The constable lugged Nick along the floor, through a narrow passage, into a small white-walled room. The only window was a horizontal slit high up on one wall. On the floor lay a stained lumpy-looking mattress with a grey blanket thrown over its foot. In the corner stood a slop pail and an earthenware bowl.

The constable banged the door shut, removed Nick's handcuffs and proceeded to strip off his clothes. Nick felt like a rag doll, floppy, with limbs made of straw.

The sergeant came in. 'Find anything?'

'Nothing.'

'I think we'll have to leave him to cool off for a few hours and then see if he's ready to talk to us. But first of all, he needs to be taught a lesson. Get up, Scotsman!'

The constable yanked him to his feet and held him while his superior delivered Nick a few more hard, well-aimed punches. He stopped when Nick passed out.

Thirteen

Nick was cold and shivering violently when he came round. His head felt like a drum, tight and hot and sore. Every part of him hurt and for a moment he could not think where he was. It was pitch dark. He was not in the cave, that was as much as he knew. The cave had a soft earth floor; the one he lay on now was hard and unyielding. Then he remembered the sergeant and the violent look of hate there had been in the man's eyes when he'd swung his fist at him. He had to adjust to the knowledge that he was locked in a cell, naked, a prisoner of the Civil Guard, though civil was the last word he would have thought of giving to his two jailers, one of whom was Isabel's father.

There had been a mattress, he seemed to remember, with a blanket lying on top. He crawled around until he felt it, then inched himself bit by bit on to the low pallet and pulled the rough blanket over him and went to sleep. His dreams were lurid and even though he was not properly conscious he was aware that he was crying out aloud. Whenever he did, he wakened with a jerk but was immediately sucked back down into a vortex of terror in which he was endlessly running, running, running, and a dog with flaring eyes like light bulbs was snapping at his heels.

When he wakened finally, the room was filled with grey light. He saw that they had taken his knapsack but had left his clothes in an untidy heap on the floor. It took him almost half an hour to dress himself, after which he had to rest. They had left him his watch, too. Nick was grateful for that, at least. His father had given it to him on his thirteenth birthday. Lifting his arm, Nick saw that the hands had stopped at seven minutes past nine. Had he forgotten to wind it? Or was that the time when the sergeant had knocked him to the floor? The watch might have been broken in the fall. He began to turn the little winder but his fingers fumbled and kept slipping. He persevered, and eventually he succeeded. He smiled when he heard its steady ticking. The sound was familiar and reassuring. Nothing else about his situation was.

He suddenly remembered that he should have some painkillers left in one of his trouser pockets, unless Manuel, the constable, had found them. He scrabbled around in the pocket and deep down in the seam his fingers encountered three round pills. He felt as if he had found gold. He eased them out and gazed at them lying in the palm of his hand before putting one into his mouth and gulping it down dry. There was water in the earthenware basin but it did not look clean and the last thing he would want was dysentery to add to his troubles. He put the remaining pills back into his pocket, pushing them down as far as they would go.

Exhausted, he lay on his back and listened. He thought he heard the vague rumble of a cart, a dog barking. Not much sound would come through that narrow slit of a window. It would be too high for him to see out and there was no chance of it offering an escape. The door, too, looked solid and he could be sure that it was firmly bolted on the other side.

As the pain receded a little he was able to think about his situation. The veterans' stories had prepared him for some of the things that might happen to him, but only partially. He had listened but, foolishly perhaps, he had not really expected such tribulations to befall him. In the end, when it had come to this, being beaten up and left naked on the floor of a prison cell, he had been alone and the pain was no less because other people had suffered similarly. But many of them had survived much worse than this, he told himself. *Always hold on to hope*, Jean-Luc had said, *whatever happens*.

The sergeant would be back and he would demand answers to questions. Nick pondered on what he should, or could, tell him. He could say that he had come to look for his father but claim that he was a Nationalist. He could give a false surname, say his family lived in Granada. He had visited cousins in Granada a couple of times and knew the city well enough to pin down a district if pressed. He didn't think the Civil Guard here in the north would be particularly interested in trying to track down his father. Why should they? They had enough going on on their own patch. He thought the punishment meted out to him had been about Isabel as much as anything else.

He thought about her for the first time since his arrest. She wouldn't have betrayed him to her father, of course she wouldn't! But she had persuaded him to stay an extra night in the cave, hadn't she, when he had wanted to leave straight away? Perhaps her father had beaten her up when she got home and made her talk. He couldn't blame her if that had been the way of it. Perhaps Pedro had changed his mind and decided to tell on her. Isabel, though, had seemed fairly sure that her brother could be bought off, since money meant so much to him.

A key was rattling in the lock. Nick's pulse quickened. Was the next interrogation to begin again so soon? He had just managed to pull himself together after the last one. The door swung open to admit the constable carrying a pitcher and a brown paper bag. He booted the door shut behind him and put the stuff on the floor.

'We're not going to let you starve, Scotsman. Sergeant Morales wants you to be in shape for another little session with him. He'll be coming in to have a chat tomorrow. Today, we are busy. We have bigger fish to fry than you. We have a report of two Americans being sighted out in the *campo*. They could have been left behind by the International Brigade. Serves them right, interfering in our war.' The man snickered and said, touching the paper bag with his toe, 'Don't eat it all at once!' He went out and once more locked the door.

There was water in the pitcher – all right to drink, Nick presumed – and in the bag, bread and olives. He ate and drank, leaving half of everything for another time and went back to his bed. Jean-Luc had advised him, if he should find himself in such a situation, to think of something definite: recite songs or verses of poetry to himself, go over the story of a novel trying to remember the names of each character, do anything other than lie, letting random, anxiety-provoking thoughts fill his mind.

Nick closed his eyes and imagined the jagged outline of a map of Scotland. He marked first of all the names of all the islands lying off the coast. He had spent many holidays with his parents in the Western Isles, as well as Orkney and Shetland to the north. His father had loved Scotland. Next came the hills and mountains: the Grampians and the Cairngorms, the two ranges he knew best. Then he marked in the hills of Wester Ross, Argyll and Perthshire, and the lower Sidlaws, Campsies and Moorfoots. He saw in his mind's eye the peaks he had climbed with his father, recalled the exhilaration he'd felt standing up there on top of the world, with the countryside stretched out before them. Lords of all they surveyed. Then he put in the major rivers: the Tweed, the Clyde, the Forth, the Tay, the Spey, the Dee, and the Don, and after that some of their tributaries. He could not remember all of them but he was pleased by how many did come to him when he concentrated. Now for the lochs: Lomond, Ness, Lochy, Oich, Linnhe, Tay, Rannoch, and others. After that he set himself to fill in the names of as many cities, towns and villages as he could remember.

By the time he had finished he felt as if he had travelled the length and breadth of Scotland. He fell asleep, and this time slept more peacefully.

The day had gone when he awoke but tonight there was a moon which sent a shaft of light through the window slit into the room. He ate some bread and olives, drank a little more water, and took another painkiller. That left him with one. He used the slop pail, rinsed his left hand in the earthenware bowl, noting that the dressing on his right was looking grubby, but it would have to do. The remaining clean ones were in his knapsack.

He stood in the middle of the floor and stretched himself, pushing his arms high above his head and out to the side, reaching as far as he could, and then walked gingerly round the room a few times, feeling his legs. He had to keep mobile. *Keep the blood circulating in your muscles.* Jean-Luc could write a manual on survival.

Having slept all day, Nick felt wide awake now. He lay on the mattress and stared at the shadows on the ceiling, listening to the silence. They said you could never have perfect silence, that there was always some ambient noise, but the quiet seemed deathly, as if everyone in the world had died. Could he hear a beetle scuffling? He was listening so intently that he might have been able to hear the proverbial pin drop. But *that* was a noise, surely it was, outside the door. He sat up.

A key was scraping in the lock, more tentatively than before, as if searching for the groove. Was it the sergeant coming to dish out more punishment? He might think it would be more effective in the middle of the night. Nick felt the trembling begin in his limbs. His eyes remained riveted on the door while it creaked slowly open. Isabel slid into the room.

'Isabel!' He sprang up.

'Shh!' She put a finger to her mouth. 'Can you walk?'

'Sort of.'

'You'll have to try.'

'But how on earth—?'

'Ask no questions now, Nick. Just come!'

He went.

Fourteen

The deserted village street looked eerie under the pale light of the moon. A ginger cat was sitting on a doorstep, its green eyes gleaming. It turned its head to watch them.

'Do you think you could carry these?' Isabel handed Nick his bedroll and knapsack. Another bedroll was strapped to her back and over one shoulder she wore a rectangular saddle-bag similar to one he'd seen a shepherd wearing. 'Let's go!' she said. He followed her as if in a dream.

Since the Civil Guard station was on the edge of the village they did not have to pass any houses. A short distance along the road they struck off into the *campo*, going in the opposite direction from Nick's old hideaway. He was still stunned by the speed at which Isabel had released him from his prison. His head buzzed with questions that would have to wait.

He managed to walk for an hour before he had to stop for a rest and a drink of water. His bottle was in his knapsack, full. Isabel had another in her shoulder bag.

'You're doing very well,' she said.

He could feel the adrenalin running in his system. He'd felt it surge the moment Isabel had said, 'Just come!'

They set off again, with her leading the way, keeping a pace or two in front of him so that he kept up his pace, too, determined not to lag behind. They reached a main road.

'Wait!' She put out a hand to hold him back. They crouched down in the undergrowth.

Something was coming. Nick felt uneasy. It could be the sergeant and his mate out on the hunt for them. His absence might have been discovered. Isabel's too. Could they have really managed to escape without being heard? It all seemed too simple. How had Isabel managed to get the key. And his bedroll and knapsack?

A vehicle came into view, its headlights fanning the road in front of it. It looked greyish in colour and was very much like an army truck.

'Don't worry,' whispered Isabel. 'They won't be looking for us.'

How could she be so sure? Her father might have phoned the nearest army base and asked them to put their security forces on alert as there was a spy on the run with his daughter.

They were about to leave their cover when they heard another vehicle coming. In the next fifteen minutes ten more army trucks rattled past. They must be on manoeuvres. Isabel and Nick waited another five minutes before they risked crossing, then they did it at top speed.

On the other side of the road the *campo* became more undulating and Nick realised from the strain on the backs of his legs that they were gaining altitude little by little. After a while they dropped down again, to a river bed. There was some water in this one, not a great deal, but enough to make them take off their shoes to ford it. Crossing through water was said to throw a dog off your scent. With luck it would thwart the wolfhound with the red eyes and evil fangs.

Nick was forced to stop at intervals to rest. As the night progressed the intervals became longer and more frequent. On one occasion when he lay down he thought he would never get up again, but he did. He felt as if Isabel was transmitting her strength to him, willing him forwards.

Most of the time there were tracks to follow, though every now and then they ran out and the terrain became wilder, strewn with boulders and stunted trees. Nick wondered if Isabel could possibly know where she was going in this dark wilderness. She was pressing on as if she had an end in sight, hesitating only when they came to a fork in the paths. She'd stop, frown, then say, 'Yes, I'm sure this is the right one.'

In more fertile parts they passed scattered habitations, small farmhouses mostly. Only one of them showed a light, and this they gave a wide berth. Near another a dog began to howl as if warning its masters of impending danger. They lay low until it had ceased.

They talked very little, even when they stopped, needing to conserve every bit of energy. On one stop Nick took the last of his painkillers.

'I have a couple more for you in my bag,' said Isabel. 'I got them from Marina. And some dressings. I'm sure your hand must need to be cleaned up.' So she had let Marina into their secret.

They moved on again. The sky was gradually taking on colour.

'Not much further,' said Isabel. 'I'd hoped to make it before dawn but I don't think we will quite.'

And then it was sunrise, with the great orange ball edging up over the horizon, climbing gradually higher and higher to flood the sky with light. It looked so beautiful they had to stop. Nick was able to see Isabel clearly now and he saw that she had cast off her mourning in favour of a blue cotton dress.

By the time the sky had become a calm azure blue, the same colour as her dress, they had arrived at their destination. Ahead of them, on the slope of a hillside, lay a ruined shepherd's hut, with no other building in sight, nor any sheep either.

'That's it,' said Isabel. Our *fonda*.' Their lodging house.

Nick staggered the last few metres and then he collapsed.

'You can rest now,' said Isabel. 'We shall be safe here.'

One wall of the hut had partially crumbled away and the door hung loose, half off its hinges, but the roof was more or less intact. There were no windows – the door when open served as one. Isabel took a stick and began beating about the straw-littered earth floor, to make sure that no snakes were lurking. Then she put down their blankets and laid out the food she had brought with her.

'We can't eat too much. We have to make it last. You won't be fit to move on for a day or two.'

'How did you know this place?'

'I used to come here with my brother Juan. It was our hideaway.'

'It's a long way from the village.'

'That's what we liked about it. It took us almost half the morning to get here, and half the evening to get back. We were faster, of course, and we were fit and didn't have heavy packs to carry. We came in summer, when the evenings were long. We walked a lot in the *campo* together, Juan and I.' Isabel's voice dropped and she gazed out through the open doorway.

Nick now asked the question he'd been bursting to ask all night. 'How did you get the key of the cell?'

'It's kept in a locked cupboard in my father's office and the key is kept in the drawer of his desk, which is always left unlocked. He doesn't expect anyone to come breaking into his office.'

Maybe not anyone, but what about his daughter? Nick could imagine his rage when he found out. It would be terrifying.

'But how did you get into the station itself? It must have been locked?'

'I took the key from the table in his bedroom.'

'Did he not notice?'

'He was sleeping.'

'But weren't you worried he'd wake up? Or your mother?'

'No.' Isabel took an olive and bit into it. 'I knew they wouldn't. My mother has to take sleeping draughts so that she can sleep. They both drink warm milk before going to bed. I put a draught in his milk too.'

'Wow!' It was all Nick could think to say. 'What about Pedro, or does he sleep soundly anyway?'

'I gave him one as well, to make certain.'

'And the dog?'

'I gave him double.'

Now Nick had to laugh.

'I had to be sure he would sleep for a long time. He's such a nasty brute.'

'And what about the constable?'

'He was on duty. My father had told me to take him in a cup of coffee earlier. I gave him a draught too. By the time I came back he was asleep.'

'Isabel, you are wonderful!' Nick then wanted to know how her father had found him in the cave. 'Was it Pedro?'

'I thought I'd been able to buy him off but he didn't go away, he hung around watching us. And when he saw you kissing me he went wild. He waited until I left you, then he came after me. He asked me how I'd dared let one of the enemy kiss me. I told you were not an enemy but he didn't believe me; he went running home ahead of me.'

'What did your father do to you? Did he beat you? He did, didn't he? Isabel, I am so sorry. And it's all because of me!'

'My bruises will heal, just as yours will.'

They might have scars to show for it afterwards, though. Nick covered his face with his hands. He could accept that he might have scars but he couldn't bear to think that Isabel would as well. She had suffered too much on his behalf.

86

'Don't blame yourself, Nick. Please! You mustn't. It won't help.'

He took his hands away to look at her. 'You are so strong, Isabel. How were you able to do all those things?'

'Nick,' she said, 'I don't think you realise just what the war has done to all of us.'

Fifteen

They slept for several hours, making up for sleep lost overnight. Nick wakened to find the hut empty and Isabel's blanket neatly rolled up on the floor. For a moment he panicked, thinking she'd gone, but then he told himself that she wouldn't have left her bedding behind. He struggled to the door. There was no sign of her. She might have gone to a spring, but no, the water-bottles were there, and when he lifted his he found it to be full. She must have been to the spring already.

She didn't come back until late in the afternoon and by then he was anxious. He was worried that something might have happened to her. He was worried that her father might somehow have found her, that the dog might not have slept all day and tracked their scent, in spite of their having crossed water.

'I just wanted to be up on the hill for a while.' Alone, she meant. In her hand she had a small posy of yellow and lilac flowers which she held to her face. She was much quieter than he had known her and he felt she had withdrawn from him.

She dressed his hand, they ate, and afterwards sat at the door to watch the sun go down. They spoke a little, commenting on the sunset, the heaviness of the air. Nick wondered if it might be the sultry weather that was affecting Isabel. He felt as if the air was pressing down on his own skull. He was not used to such heat. He preferred the cooler breezes of northern Scotland in summer. But perhaps Isabel's change of mood had nothing at all to do with the weather. Perhaps she was regretting what she had done. She had burned her boats, after all. It would be impossible for her to go home now, probably ever.

The sky in the west had turned a molten red and ochre, smudged with long trails of purple cloud. It was a troubled, menacing sky.

'I wish it would break,' said Nick, trying to dry his forehead with the back of his hand. He felt hot and sticky and there were mosquitoes about. They were attacking him as if with little sharp knives, whereas they seemed to leave Isabel alone.

'A storm will come,' she said. 'Later.'

They were woken in the early hours of the morning by loud claps of thunder and frantic flashes of forked lightning. The storm raged for two hours. Nick had never seen such a violent one; it was as if someone up there was bent on destroying the earth. It was disturbing and frightening, yet, at the same time, enthralling. Gradually the thunder moved further and further away until it was only a rumble in the distance. And then came the rain, torrential, unremitting, blinding, shutting them off from the outside world.

'There will be flash floods,' said Isabel. 'In the dried-up river beds.'

Nick knew that flash floods could be dangerous; they were capable of sweeping away houses, villages, people, animals, anything in their path. This was a country of extremes. Extremes of intense heat and freezing cold, of drought and deep floods. Extremes of passion, too. Nick knew that from his father, who was much more volatile than his mother, and more impulsive. When he had decided to go off to fight in Spain's Civil War he had wanted to leave immediately. Nick and his mother had gone to see him off at the railway station. He remembered the terrible moment when his father had put his head out of the window to wave for the last time and the aching sense of emptiness he'd been left with when, finally, the train, chugging slowly, had disappeared round the bend, taking his father away.

'Let's go home,' his mother had said.

They had gone home and stayed there until, in March this year, they had heard that the Civil War had ended, and then they had set off for France.

Nick sat in the tiny stone hut with all these memories and thoughts drifting through his mind, watching the curtain of rain falling. At home, it seldom rained all day; it might be wet in the morning but would clear up later. This rain looked set for the day.

He turned his head to look at Isabel. She was crying.

'What is it? What's wrong, Isabel?'

She shook her head.

'You must tell me!'

'I'm worried about my mother.' He could only just make out what she was saying above the drumming of the rain.

He moved closer but did not touch her. The only thing he could think to say was that he was sorry, and that would sound lame. And he had said it before.

'I feel terrible that I've left her. She needs me.'

Guilt consumed Nick again, like a fiery furnace. If Isabel had not met him she would be at home looking after her mother. He knew even less now what to say. He hated to see her crying like this. Tentatively he put an arm round her shoulders, ready to withdraw it if she shrank from him, but she did not. She allowed herself to lean against his shoulder and after a while she dried her tears. They stayed like that for a long time, silently watching the rain.

It was still raining when they settled down again, but when they wakened finally they found it had stopped. The air smelt clean and fresh, with scents of grass and rosemary and lavender brought out by the rain.

'We're going to have to move on,' said Isabel, when they had eaten the last of their food. 'We won't find anything to eat round here. There might be the odd berry but nothing more.'

'Where to, have you any idea?'

'None. I don't know the *campo* further on. We'll just have to start walking until we hit a road.'

Going into civilisation might be dangerous, but staying up here to starve wouldn't do them any good, either. They would have to take a chance.

Nick was feeling stronger and his headaches were lessening. The blows inflicted by the sergeant had caused lurid bruises to flower on his face and arms, but the pain was no longer severe. He thought of the man always as 'the sergeant', not as 'Isabel's father'.

'Are you sure you want to come on with me, Isabel?' he asked.

'I can't very well go back, can I?'

He acknowledged that.

'It was my own decision to come. You didn't ask me to do it.'

She might have felt she'd had no choice, since it was her brother who had betrayed him.

'I'd have had to leave home eventually, anyway,' she said. 'Living with my father, and my brother, was slowly killing me. They could be cruel, both of them, each in their own way. They treated me like a slave. That is how they see women.'

'And your mother, how will she manage?'

'She has a sister in the village who will stand by her. Perhaps she'll live with her.'

They rolled up their blankets, filled their water-bottles, and set off.

After walking for some time they reached a road, a minor, unpaved one, much potholed, greatly in need of repair, like most roads in the country, but at least it was a sign that there might be life near by. Their heels kicked up little clouds of dust as they walked. It looked as if it had not rained here for weeks. A mule cart rattled past, followed by a motor cycle. Shortly afterwards they came upon a house, a poor affair. A woman pegging out washing on the strip of ground at the side stopped to stare at them but did not return their 'Buenas tardes'. Good afternoon. They felt her eyes on their backs. A man passing on a donkey, his feet swaddled in rags, did grunt in response to their greeting, as if to say, 'I see you there, I acknowledge your presence as fellow travellers on the road, but don't expect me to be friendly since I don't know who you are or where you're from or what you're doing.'

'They're bound to wonder about us,' said Isabel. 'But I think most people just want to mind their own business these days.'

Ahead they saw the beginnings of a village.

'What do you think?' asked Nick.

'We have to risk it.'

They soon saw that the village was very small, with not even a sign to identify it, but it did have a shop, not much more than a hole in the wall. Every village seemed to have one like it. Nick had no money since all of his had been taken from him.

'I have my savings,' said Isabel. 'I took it back from Pedro when I realised what he'd done. He'd broken the contract.'

They pushed through a beaded curtain and went inside the shop. For a moment, after leaving the glare of the sun, they could see nothing, then gradually they made out shelves against the wall, virtually bare, and a few empty glass jars on the counter.

The woman behind the counter was not going to be friendly, that was plain. She was eyeing them stonily.

'Buenas tardes, señora,' said Isabel. 'Have you any bread?'

'No bread.'

'Cheese?'

'No cheese.'

Isabel pointed to a tin on the top shelf. 'Olives?'

'Only for customers. Regular customers.'

'Have you anything we could buy?'

The woman shrugged. 'Stomach powder,' she said, indicating a dusty packet on the shelf behind her.

'We don't need that.'

The woman stared them down until they left.

'Not much of a shopping trip, was it!' said Nick, trying to sound cheerful.

They were tired and hungry and there would probably not be another shop in the village. They walked on and after the houses ran out they came to an inn, a low ramshackle building up an earthen path. The door was standing open.

'Shall we see if they can give us something to eat?' Isabel led the way in.

They found themselves in a small dark lobby, buzzing with flies. Off it, to the right, was a door which, when they pushed it open, revealed a bar, equally small and dark, with a dirt floor. Two men in grimy overalls sat at one of the two small tables, playing dominoes. They looked up momentarily at the new arrivals. Behind the bar, a bald man wearing a stained canvas apron was in the middle of pouring a shot of brandy into a glass. For himself. He tossed it back before addressing Isabel and Nick.

'*Buenas tardes, señorita. Señor!*' Was he actually *welcoming* them? They could hardly believe it. 'What brings you to these parts?'

'We are on our way to Madrid to visit our grandparents,' said Isabel. They had decided that this would be their story.

'You are walking all the way?'

'Well, no, we hope not. We hope we may get a lift with someone.'

'I wish I had grandchildren who would come to visit me! Well, now, what can I do for you two young people?'

'We would like something to eat, that is if you have anything.'

'I expect I can find something.' The man came out from behind the bar and gave each of them his hand in turn. 'Call me Pepe! And you?'

'María and Paco,' said Isabel.

'Now, María and Paco, what about some soup, eh? And a tasty morsel of nice juicy blood sausage? Come into the kitchen!'

The soup was bubbling in a cauldron, looking and smelling rather like a witch's brew. *Bubble, bubble, toil and trouble.* The jingle from *Macbeth* ran through Nick's head, though there didn't seem to be much sign of trouble here and perhaps not too much toil either. There was a big wooden table in the centre of the room which looked no cleaner than the floor. Pepe seated them at it and, with a flourish, ladled out two large bowlfuls of soup. They dipped their spoons in straight away. The liquid was greasy and tasted of cabbage that had been too long boiled but, even so, it was welcome on their empty stomachs. Pepe also produced a hunk of bread and a piece of reddish rubbery sausage that took a lot of chewing.

'It's good?'

They nodded.

The door opened and the two domino players came in.

'Off home?' said Pepe.

The men cast a glance at the two strangers seated at the table, said '*Adiós*' to Pepe, and went out into the yard. A moment later horses' hooves were heard clattering on the cobbles.

'You have no horse to stable?' asked Pepe.

'No,' said Nick. 'None.'

'You are walking?'

They didn't have time to answer before a bell rang in the lobby outside. Pepe left them to answer it. Isabel and Nick were immediately on the alert again. They laid down their spoons. But the person talking to Pepe appeared to be a traveller like themselves; he was asking for overnight accommodation.

Pepe brought the man into the kitchen. He was small and dressed in dark-blue overalls with a cap pulled down low on his forehead. 'This is Cristóbal, who is to be my guest tonight. He comes this way from time to time. And here we have María and Paco!' Pepe presented them with a flourish.

'Brother and sister?' asked Cristóbal.

'Don't you think they look alike?' said Pepe.

Cristóbal joined them at the table and a bowl of soup was set in front of him. He asked if they were staying the night as well.

'You have taken the very words from my mouth!' said Pepe. 'I was just going to ask them that. My rates are very cheap. You will not find better.'

Isabel looked at Nick and he nodded. They were too tired to move on and look for shelter. The innkeeper seemed friendly. Of course, one could never be sure, but it was yet another chance they would have to take.

Sixteen

The sleeping accommodation at the inn consisted of two low-ceilinged lofts, each ventilated by a small unglazed window. Nick, who was about ten centimetres taller than Cristóbal, was unable to stand upright.

'There are some advantages in being small,' said Cristóbal, whose cap just cleared the ceiling. He had kept it on throughout the evening. He sat down on his straw mattress and pulled off his boots, releasing a strong smell of stale feet into the room. Then he lay back, with his hands linked behind his head.

Nick, aware that his own feet would not smell any better, proceeded to do the same. He had a huge broken blister on one heel and by now had run out of plasters. Pepe might have some surgical spirit. He was being very kind to them; he'd given them each a large glass of sherry after their meal, on the house. 'Drink it down, it'll do you good. You look like two coiled springs ready to go ping!' After they'd drunk it down he refilled their glasses and by the time they'd come up to bed they'd been feeling woozy. Pepe had said it would give them a good night's sleep.

'Hope I won't snore,' said Cristóbal.

'Shouldn't think I'd hear you,' said Nick.

'I've been in a room with five men, all snoring their heads off, like trains. Nearly bored a hole in my skull.'

Nick was about to lie down himself when the bell rang downstairs. They heard Pepe, humming a tune, go to answer it.

'Ah, *buenas noches, señores*!' Good evening, gentlemen!

'Someone's late coming in,' said Nick, his anxiety returning.

The men at the door were not looking for accommodation.

'It's the Guard!' said Cristóbal, shooting upright.

Nick sat very still. Isabel was in the other loft, at the back of the building, and might not hear what was going on. Should he go through and warn her? They couldn't make a run for it, though – jump out of the window, or anything like that. Any such crazy action was out of the question.

The guards were asking about a truck that they wanted to inspect.

'That's mine,' groaned Cristóbal. 'I'd better go down.'

When he'd gone Nick crept through to Isabel's room to tell her what was happening. 'But don't worry, it's Cristóbal's truck they're interested in.' He went back and stood on the landing so that he could hear what was going on downstairs. The voices were no longer audible. They must have moved up to the road where the truck was parked. Nick hoped Cristóbal was not going to land in trouble.

A few minutes later the guards and Cristóbal were back in the hall below.

'Everything all right?' asked Pepe.

'Seems to be,' one of the guards replied.

'Good, good. My lodgers can always be relied on to be on the right side of the law. They would never flout it.'

'What about yourself, Pepe?'

'You know Pepe better than that!'

'Oh yes, we know Pepe! You haven't seen a boy and a girl, have you?'

Nick thought his heart would stop.

'What kind of a boy and girl? There are a number in the village. My sister's girl is thirteen and she has a boy of ten—'

'Girl's called Isabel Morales. Sixteen. Long straight black hair. Dark eyes. She's the daughter of a sergeant in the Guard.'

'Ah, ha! Run off with her boyfriend, has she?'

'Some boyfriend! Girls can be so stupid. He's a spy. A Scotsman. Name of Nicolás Maceentos. He's tall, about one metre eighty, dark hair, brown eyes, looks Spanish, speaks Spanish.'

'I cannot say I have come across a Scottish spy. Does he wear that skirt they favour in his country?'

Thank you, Pepe, Nick whispered silently.

'Hardly! Not if he wants to pass as a spy. We'd see him coming then, wouldn't we?'

'True, officer. Your mind is sharper than mine, that is obvious. That is why I am only a poor innkeeper.'

'Lay off the soft soap, Pepe, and keep your eyes open in case they should happen to wander into your field of vision. How about one for the road before we go?'

'Of course, *señores*! Forgive my lack of hospitality. Do please come in and grace my humble bar!'

The voices moved from the hall below, into the bar.

A moment later Cristóbal came back upstairs. 'Bastards! I had to give them a couple of skins.' Then, resettling his cap, lay down again. Nick stayed where he was, sitting on his mattress, listening for the sound of the guards taking their leave.

'*Buenas noches, señores*.' Pepe's voice floated out into the night after them. 'Sleep well.' Then he closed the door and threw the bolt. 'And may you never waken again,' he added softly.

Relieved, Nick lay down.

'Shall I put out the candle?' asked Cristóbal.

'Please.'

Cristóbal leant over and with a puff extinguished the candle. A quiff of acrid smoke rose in the air.

'Pepe could do to get himself a couple more lamps. One of these days a drunk's going to knock a candle over and burn the whole place down.'

The unglazed window was letting in light from the moon. Nick stared at the shadows on the ceiling, wondering if he would be able to sleep. He was sweating a little again from the fever.

'Are you going far, lad?' asked Cristóbal.

'South.'

'I could give you a lift as far as Madrid. You and the girl.'

'Would you?'

'I'm making an early start. I'll wake you.'

'Thank you! Thank you very much!'

'Glad to help.'

'Cristóbal, do you think it's all right for us to stay? I wouldn't want to get Pepe into trouble?'

'Sure. Just go to sleep. They won't be back. Not tonight anyway.'

Nick was drifting off when he heard a loud bang. He sat up at once. 'Was that a *shot*?' There came another, and then another, in rapid succession.

'You often hear shots in the night,' said Pepe. 'That's when they carry out their executions. Just be glad it's not you.'

It was a long time before Nick did sleep.

Cristóbal roused Nick while it was still dark and he went to waken Isabel. 'We're getting a lift to Madrid. I have the address of a contact there, someone who can help.'

When he returned Cristóbal was stripping off his shirt, having first removed his cap. Nick saw that he was bald and his scalp criss-crossed with hideous scars, as were his back and shoulders. War wounds? He wouldn't ask.

Cristóbal also had a scattering of small red lumps round his waistband.

Nick scratched his own waist. 'I think I've got some bites too.'

'Bed bugs. These old *fondas* are jumping with them. Here, take this soap and see how many you can swat.'

Nick counted ten black marks before washing them off in the basin of water on the dresser, but it was not likely he would have got them all.

Pepe was already up, brewing something that tasted vaguely of coffee. 'It's good, eh? I made it with acorns. Who could tell the difference!' They were each given a small piece of bread to dunk in it. And then they were ready for the road. Cristóbal paid for his accommodation and left to check his truck.

'How much do we owe you, Pepe?' asked Isabel.

'Nothing. It's on the house.' Isabel protested but Pepe refused to take a single peseta. 'You only had some soup and a little piece of sausage. No, keep your money. You might need it. With Cristóbal it's different – he gets some money from his company for his lodging.'

Pepe saw them out on to the road, after doing a scout around first to make sure the coast was clear. 'Not a sign. They don't usually get out of their beds this early, especially when they've been busy in the night. You heard them?'

They nodded.

Nick held out his hand. 'Thank you for everything, Pepe. I wish we could repay you.'

'Some day, some day! When you are rich and have made your fortune and are driving past in your big motor, you can stop in to say hello to Pepe the poor innkeeper and pay me. We have to help each other when we can, no?'

Isabel gave him a hug.

'She is beautiful, eh?' Pepe winked at Nick. 'You are a lucky young man.' So Pepe had guessed that they were not brother and sister. Perhaps anyone observing them closely would realise that. Isabel had turned her head away so that Nick could not see her face.

Cristóbal was holding open the back door of his truck. It was not much more than a van and it promised a rocky ride, especially with the roads being in such poor condition.

'Sorry about the smell, but at least they make a soft cushion.' The interior was full of animal skins, some goat, mostly sheep. Isabel and Nick climbed in and Cristóbal closed the door.

The journey was difficult, what with the itching of their flea bites, the jolting of the truck, the lack of light and air and, more than anything else, the overpowering stench of the skins. Nick was thinking they might suffocate before they reached Madrid, when Cristóbal opened the door and released them into the fresh air. They were in the middle of flat countryside, with no buildings in their immediate sight except for a broken-down windmill with sagging arms. They staggered over to the verge at the side of the road and Isabel promptly vomited into the undergrowth.

'Sorry about that,' she muttered when she'd straightened up.

Cristóbal was concerned. Did they still want to carry on with him? He'd understand if they didn't.

Nick and Isabel consulted but soon realised that their only other option would be to start walking again. To try for another lift could be tricky. 'We've got to go on,' said Isabel, whose colour was returning after a drink of water and a break in the sunshine. Nick asked Cristóbal if they could stop more often and he agreed to take a five-minute break every hour. And after four hours they'd make a longer stop to eat the bread and cheese Pepe had given them.

The hours passed painfully slowly. Nick tried to think about Scotland but failed. He tried not to scratch but he failed on that score too. After their lunch stop they wondered if they'd be able to get back in among the foul-smelling skins, but they did.

When at last they arrived in Madrid they almost fell out of the back of the truck. Once they'd thanked Cristóbal he took off straight away, leaving them in a street of high, dark tenements which blotted out the sun but trapped the heat. At the far end the buildings dwindled away into a sad heap of rubble. A family was camping in the ruins of one that had half collapsed. The rooms were open to the elements and visible to the world. The floors lay at a tilted angle. Rotting sandbags littered the pavement. Children played in a crater in the middle of the road. They seemed to be playing at boats, pretending they were sailing on a hard grey sea. Their high-pitched cries filled the air. On a step sat a man with both trouser legs pinned back at the knee. Close by, another leant against a wall, a pair of crutches parked beside him. Both men wore black armbands.

Isabel and Nick stood, debating which way to go. Nick knew his contact's address but had no idea where that would be. Madrid was a very big city. Isabel had been here once, to visit her favourite aunt, her mother's younger sister, but that was a few years ago.

'We could try to make our way there if we're stuck,' she said.

'You could, but I don't think it would be a good idea for me.'

'Aunt Ana would be on my side. She dislikes my father.'

Nick wondered if anyone liked him, even his wife. He did not tell Isabel what he was thinking, of course. Much of the time he had no idea what went on in her mind. Sometimes he was tempted to ask her, but he never had. She was not the kind of girl to chatter and spill out everything that came into her head. But they did not have to talk to feel comfortable together.

Some of the passers-by were wrinkling their noses and giving them a wide berth. They had to hope that the smell on their clothes would gradually fade in the fresh air. Not that the air was all that fresh. A nearby factory chimney was belching out smoke.

They began to walk. They turned into another, similar street. A gaggle of children, some of the ones who'd been playing in the crater, had come after them. They were barefoot and their clothes hung in rags. They danced like dervishes on the pavement in front of them, flicking their fingers and holding out cupped palms. '*Por favor, por favor!*' Please, please!

Isabel and Nick shook their heads and held on to their knapsacks and bedrolls. 'We have nothing,' they said. *Nada.* The children did not believe it but gradually they dropped back.

Isabel stopped the next passer-by. The woman, who was elderly, put her head to the side and a hand to her ear. Isabel had to shout the address out three times, which made Nick feel nervous. The woman finally said, 'Never heard of it,' and shuffled on, her empty shopping bag trailing on the ground behind her.

A man appeared then at their elbow, saying he'd happened to overhear and that he knew the street. His mother lived there. It was only ten to fifteen minutes' walk. He was going that way so he escorted them, chatting, asking where they came from and if they knew Madrid. They began to feel a little uneasy, thinking he was asking too many questions. They were relieved when he said, '*Adiós,*' and left them to go into a building.

They found the street, lined, again, with tenements. A new swarm of barefoot children came buzzing about them like bees round a honeycomb. *Por favor! Por favor!* Once more, the cry went up.

'Seventy-two,' Nick mouthed to Isabel over the tops of the children's heads. 'Top floor.'

A few of the children followed them into the dark stairway but gave up before they reached the fourth floor. Isabel and Nick kept on going. Different smells assailed them here: a combination of cat, rancid cooking oil and communal lavatories.

On the top landing there were two doors, both scabby, neither of which bore a name. One had a spyhole, roughly carved into the wood.

'I think that should be it,' said Nick.

He waited a moment before raising his knuckles. It was nerve-racking, this moment of arrival at what was assumed to be a 'safe house', when nothing could ever be totally safe. The contact might have moved away or, worse, been taken away by the Guard or the secret police.

'What if it's the wrong one?' asked Isabel.

'Then we run,' said Nick.

Seventeen

Nick knocked, giving three short taps and two longer ones. Isabel waited beside him, with her head cocked to one side. Someone was on the other side of the door; they could sense it. Nick took a step back so that whoever was peering into the little hole would be able to have a good look at him.

The door opened a couple of inches, secured by a chain. 'Yes?' No one was visible, but the voice was a man's.

'I'm looking for Salvador.'

'Salvador? Should I know him?'

'I think so.'

'So, who are you?'

'The son of Sebastián Torres.'

'Should I know him as well?'

'I've been told so.'

'By whom?'

'Jean-Luc the Frenchman.'

'And this Sebastián Torres, where is he from?'

Isabel was looking uneasy and mouthing, 'Let's go,' but Nick held up his hand, knowing as he did that it was necessary to go through this interrogation. 'Scotland,' he said to the man behind the door.

'You say you are his son?'

'Yes. My name is Nicolás. My mother's name is Mairi.'

'All right.' The chain rattled, and the door opened. A man in his early forties, about the same age as Nick's father, stood on the threshold. He recoiled for a moment, then he welcomed them and invited them in.

'This is my friend Isabel,' said Nick.

'Isabel, I am pleased to meet you.' Salvador inclined his head.

'We won't shake hands,' she said and explained why they smelt as they did.

'It can't have been a very sweet journey!' Salvador laughed and said that he would find them clean clothes. 'Please, do come in.'

He led the way. He walked with a pronounced limp. Half the men in Spain seemed wounded, one way or another. The apartment was small, consisting only of a bedroom and a living-room with a small kitchenette off. The window was wide open, letting in the noise of city traffic and the children shouting in the street below. In spite of that it was very close in the room.

Straight away Nick said, 'Salvador, I wonder if you can help me? I'm trying to trace my father. Would you have any news of him?'

'Not recently, I'm afraid. The last time I saw him was at the battle of the River Ebro. I was there when he was wounded.'

'He was *wounded*?' Nick felt his heart begin to race.

'Why don't you sit down, both of you, and I'll make us some coffee, or what passes for it these days. Chicory and sawdust, I think. At best. You look as if you need a pick-up.'

'I don't think we should sit,' said Isabel, looking down at her skirt.

'One moment,' Salvador disappeared into the bedroom and came back with trousers and a shirt for Nick, and a skirt and blouse for Isabel. 'These are my wife's. She is not as tall as you but perhaps they will do.' He showed them the bathroom. 'We have no hot water but at least we do have water. There have been times when we have not.'

They took turns to wash and change, and to rid themselves of some more fleas. Isabel went first. By the time Nick had dressed the coffee was waiting for them.

Salvador said he hoped his wife would bring some food when she came home. She'd gone to the market on her way to work. 'I've not been able to find work myself.' He made a wry face. 'For men like me who fought on the wrong side it's almost impossible.'

'So you were with my father?' prompted Nick, who could wait no longer. 'At the battle of the Ebro, you said? When was that?'

'Last autumn sometime. October, yes, I think it began in October.' Salvador pursed his lips. 'It was a battle we looked like winning for a while. That's how it goes. Then the Nationalists came back on the offensive. They bombarded us mercilessly. They had more guns, more aircraft, more everything. They had Italian support. We didn't have much chance but we fought on into November. Then the first of the winter snows came. It was grim.' His voice cracked. He drank a mouthful of coffee and looked broodingly over the rim of his mug into space, forgetting them for a moment.

Nick waited, daring almost not to breathe, his eyes fixed on Salvador's face.

'There weren't many of us left,' Salvador went on. 'We were cold and hungry. Morale was low. What could you expect? Before long we had to withdraw from the right bank of the river. We knew the game was up at that point. It was during the retreat that Sebastián was wounded.'

'Badly?'

'Quite badly.'

'*No!*'

'His right leg was shot up and it looked like he had chest injuries. Whole place was going mad. It was sheer chaos. Shells were exploding all round us. Our emergency hospital was trying to evacuate. Ambulances were doing their best to take the wounded off, but they couldn't cope. There were hundreds of them, thousands. It was a nightmare.'

'And my father—' Nick swallowed. 'What happened to him after that?'

'Another soldier and myself, between us, we managed to drag him off the field.'

'So you saved his life, Salvador?'

'I don't know that, Nicolás. I'm not sure if he will have survived his injuries. We did manage to get him into an ambulance. It was the last I saw of him, being driven off.'

'You heard nothing after that?'

'There was no way to find out.'

'I suppose you wouldn't know anyone else who was in the ambulance? The driver, even?'

'Oh yes, I knew the driver. Carlos Cortes was his name. He was an old mate of mine. That was how I persuaded him to take Sebastián. He had a full load as it was. He let me put your father on the floor.'

'And Carlos?'

'We've not been in touch since the war ended. Who knows if he'll be alive or dead. So many didn't make it.'

They'd been so absorbed that they'd not heard the outer door of the apartment opening. A small stocky woman came bustling into the room and Salvador introduced his wife Eugenia. She set down her shopping bags to offer them her hand. It was a strong hand. This was a woman who would not let herself be pushed around. She took over. She dumped their filthy clothes straight into a sinkful of water and began to scrub them on a board with a bar of hard yellow soap, waving aside their protests. When she'd finished, she put the clothes through a mangle and, after giving them a good shake, pegged them on to a line and strung them out of the window to dangle above the street.

'They'll be dry by morning. You are going to stay, of course! We can only offer you the floor, though.'

Nick relaxed. It was good to be for a while in the company of someone who was taking charge and making decisions. And this little flat high above the street felt like a safe haven.

Meanwhile, Salvador had been unpacking Eugenia's shopping bags and was laying out the food on the big well-scrubbed wooden table in the centre of the living-room. Bread, cheese, sausage, olives, tomatoes. Isabel and Nick could scarcely believe their eyes. It was a feast.

'My wife is a wonderful shopper. If there is anything going in the market, she will be sure to find it. And to sweet-talk the stall holders into selling it to her!'

'He can talk sweetly himself, can't you hear him, my Salvador?' Eugenia smiled, then invited Nick and Isabel to take seats at the table.

Salvador filled their glasses with red wine from a pottery pitcher. '*Salud*!' he raised his glass and they echoed the toast. Good health. 'We are delighted to have you here as our guests.'

'We are very grateful,' said Nick.

'Eat, eat!' urged Eugenia.

They obeyed.

Salvador brought up the name of Carlos Cortes.

'Ah yes, Carlos,' mused Eugenia. 'We have many good memories of him. He'd come to Madrid for a weekend sometimes and he'd stay with us. He liked a bit of nightlife, did Carlos. We'd have a few drinks in the bars and then go dancing till morning. All that is gone now.' She sighed.

'I don't suppose you'd have any idea where I could find him?' asked Nick.

'He lives in Málaga,' said Salvador. 'Or he did, before the war. I don't know if we'd still have his address, do you, Eugenia?'

'I'm fairly sure I could find it.'

'Really?' Nick felt like throwing his arms round her.

'Eugenia never throws anything away,' said Salvador. 'She is the most practical woman I have ever known in my whole life.'

'You had better not let your mother hear you say that!' retorted Eugenia.

After they'd eaten she brought out an old chocolate box with a flamenco dancer on its cover. 'It was Carlos who brought me these chocolates. Good ones they were, too.' She rummaged among a number of cards. 'Here we are, the address of Señor Carlos Cortes. I told you I'd find it!'

'Does he live on his own?' asked Nick.

'No, with his mother. Your father must have told you that Spanish men love their mothers so much they find it difficult to leave home?'

Nick laughed. It was good to laugh even though, deep down, he was trying to come to terms with the knowledge that his father might not still be alive.

'Nick's father left his mother,' Isabel pointed out. 'He went all the way to Scotland to marry his bride.'

'He was brave,' said Eugenia, which made them laugh again.

They had a good evening with Eugenia and Salvador, who said they were welcome to stay as long as they liked. Nick wished they could spend a few more days with these kind people but it was out of the question, for him, at least. He had to press on. He must head south, to Málaga, to find Carlos Cortes.

For Isabel, it was a different matter. The journey was his, not hers. He would not blame her if she were to opt for staying in Madrid in the shelter of her favourite aunt's home.

Eighteen

The night was stiflingly hot again and on such a night sleep did not come easily. Nick wondered if Isabel was awake. She lay on the other side of the room, under the open window, where there was a slight, a very slight, breeze. The sounds of the streets carried on into the small hours. This city never seemed to stop. Nick lay listening to the hourly, and sometimes quarter-hourly, striking of church clocks, the buzz and backfiring of motor cycles, the blare of horns, the shouts of people still abroad, the banging of doors, the clattering of feet on stairways. He lay, half listening, and thinking about his father. His mother, too.

In the morning he would write to her. He had no idea if the letter would get through to her or not, but he would try, anyway. The postal service must be in disarray. They had heard only once from his father during the war. The envelope had been creased and dirty, as if it had been in battle itself. The message inside had said, 'I'm fine. Don't worry.' Nick's mother had said, 'What else would he say?' But, even so, receiving the letter had been important. It had been a link between him and them.

'Nick?' Isabel's voice reached him. 'Are you asleep?'

'No. I thought you were?'

'It's difficult. I keep thinking.'

'Me, too.'

They each had their separate thoughts, their separate worries. And perhaps soon they would have to go their separate ways.

He wondered how she felt, being among Republicans, people who had fought on the opposite side to her family. Her brother might have been killed in battle by Salvador. Or by Nick's own father. Had that thought occurred to her? Perhaps it had. When they had been talking about the war, he and Salvador and Eugenia, Isabel had been very quiet.

'I'm sorry about your father,' she said. 'But he may be all right, you know. The ambulance may have got him to a hospital.'

Nick knew that there would not have been much chance of that. His father had been in a Republican ambulance. The Republicans had been on the retreat, fleeing for their lives. The hospitals at that stage would have been in the hands of the victors, the Nationalists.

'Don't give up hope,' urged Isabel.

'No.'

He could not bring himself to say, 'Will you come with me to Málaga to look for Carlos Cortes?' It seemed too much to ask. Instead he said, 'I expect you would like to see your aunt?'

'Very much,' she said. 'I am very fond of her. Try to sleep now, Nick.'

'You too.'

They said good-night and he turned over and managed, after a while, to sleep.

In the morning, at breakfast, he told his hosts that he must move on.

'And how do you propose to get to Málaga?' asked Eugenia, who was on late shift today at the shoe factory where she worked.

'Get a lift perhaps.'

'Not so easy,' said Salvador. 'There aren't all that many trucks on the road and the Guard search most of them.'

'Walk then, if necessary.'

'It's more than an afternoon's walk! It's several hundred kilometres.'

'What about the train?' suggested Eugenia. The railways were not very reliable at present, parts of the track had suffered bomb damage, but it might be worth trying. Some trains did appear to be running. The problem was papers. Anyone travelling by train would certainly be asked to produce them.

'Leave it with me,' Salvador got up. 'I'll be gone for a couple of hours.'

'Be careful now, Salvador!' warned Eugenia.

'Am I not always careful?' He gave her a smile and left before she could answer.

'Where has he gone, Eugenia?' asked Nick. 'I hope he won't be taking a risk on our behalf.'

'Ask no questions. It's better that way.'

Nick asked Eugenia if she could let him have a sheet of paper and envelope. 'I want to write to my mother.'

'Of course.' She fetched it for him.

He wrote a brief note, telling his mother that he was on his way south, that he was fine, and she was not to worry. Eugenia gave him a stamp.

'I'm going out to do a little shopping. If you would like to, you could come with me, Nicolás, and post your letter. Perhaps Isabel can stay and look after the apartment? I think it might be too noticeable if I were to go out with both of you.'

Isabel said that she did not mind at all. Eugenia lifted her shopping bag and Nick followed her down the stairs. On the second flight they met a neighbour, a woman with a stooped back and frizzled grey hair.

'Ah, Eugenia, so you do have visitors staying with you!' The woman's little button eyes raked Nick. 'We thought we heard voices in your apartment. I said to Alberto, "I wonder who can that be with Eugenia and Salvador?" You see, my hearing is not too bad yet!'

'Your hearing is excellent, Lidia. As good as a little child's.'

'So, who is this handsome young man?'

'The son of an old friend from Toledo.'

'Which old friend is that?'

'You would not know her. We must go now, Lidia, or there will be nothing left in the market.'

The neighbour stood aside reluctantly.

'Nosey old so-and-so,' muttered Eugenia as they continued down the stairs. 'Nothing much goes past her or Alberto. They keep their door ajar half the day in case they might miss anything.'

'Can you trust them?' Nick asked when they were out in the street.

Eugenia raised her arms in a shrug. 'Who knows?' After they had walked a little way she said, 'How long have you known Isabel?'

'Not long, I suppose, in terms of days or weeks. Though it feels like ages.' *It feels like I've always known her*, he thought. 'Why?' he asked.

'I was just wondering. I noticed that she was very quiet when we spoke of the war. Once or twice she frowned and looked away.'

'She is totally trustworthy,' he said swiftly.

'I will take your word for it.'

'You can!'

'Don't be annoyed with me, Nicolás. It is best to question everyone.'

'I know.'

Nick posted his letter and Eugenia did her shopping and then they returned to the apartment to find Isabel cleaning the kitchenette. Eugenia chided her, saying she didn't have to do that, she was a guest.

'I have to do something. I couldn't just sit here. And I was glad to do it.'

There was still no sign of Salvador though he had been gone for more than two hours.

'He'll be talking,' said Eugenia. 'I know him. They say women gossip, but men are good at it too!'

Nevertheless, when his key was heard in the lock, she was obviously relieved.

'I've had a successful outing,' he announced, looking well pleased with himself. He produced an envelope from his pocket. 'Papers for the two of you.'

'Salvador!' Nick shook his head with admiration. 'How on earth did you manage it?'

'I have friends. We help each other.'

Salvador gave a set each to Nick and Isabel.

'Not bad likenesses,' commented Eugenia, taking a look at the photographs.

'My friend had a few to choose from. Young men and women with dark hair are not too difficult. The quality of the pictures is poor so no one would know the difference unless they were to study them under a magnifying glass, which is not very likely.'

Nick was to take on the identity of Rinaldo Rosso, aged eighteen, native of Borges, a factory worker. Isabel was to become his sister Claudia, aged seventeen. Were they real people, Nick wondered. If so, what had happened to them? Better not to ask.

'You can both pass for a year or two older,' said Salvador. 'If you are asked if you fought in the war, Nick, you can say you were badly wounded at Teruel, on the Nationalist side, of course, and sent home.'

'And if they ask why we're going to Málaga?'

'You are going to visit your grandparents, Juan and Sofía Rosso. I have an address here for you to memorise.'

'What if they were to check it?'

'Records like that are not easy to check. So many were lost in the air raids. And Málaga is a long way from here.'

'I have Carlos's address for you to memorise as well,' put in Eugenia.

'It may not still be standing, of course,' warned

116

Salvador. 'Málaga was staunchly Republican and so was heavily bombed by the Italians. We heard that thousands fled during the raids and took the coast road eastwards.'

'What a state our poor country is in!' Eugenia shook her head. 'Our side did its share of destruction, too, though – we shouldn't forget that – burning convents and churches.'

'That was terrible!' exclaimed Isabel. 'Desecrating holy places.'

'It wasn't good,' agreed Eugenia, 'but, as you know, the Church was supporting the Fascist Nationalists.'

'That doesn't excuse it,' Isabel came back sharply.

'No, of course not. But in war people do things they would not do in peace.'

'So,' said Salvador, coming in to defuse the argument, 'you are travelling to Málaga to find out if your grandparents are all right. You are clear about that?'

'You've thought of everything!' said Nick.

'One has to. You can come unstuck so easily on details. Stick to your story and don't vary it. While I was out I went to the station and found that there should be a train going to Seville tonight. Not guaranteed, of course, but it seems probable.'

'Seville?' said Eugenia.

'From Seville it's not too far to Málaga. I managed to get a couple of tickets.' Salvador produced them from his pocket.

'You're like a magician, Salvador,' said Nick.

'No more tricks,' Salvador slapped his pockets. 'They are empty now.'

'I don't know how I can ever thank you.'

'Don't try.'

'The only thing,' Nick said, hesitating, 'is, well, I'm not very sure if Isabel' – he turned to look at her – 'will want to come with me or not.'

Nineteen

The lighting in the station was poor, which from their point of view was an advantage. Some bulbs were not lit at all, others glowed weakly. In between lay pools of darkness. A smell of acrid smoke hung in the air. They followed the faceless crowd surging along the platform looking for space on the night train to Seville. At least there was a train. Most compartments were full to overflowing, but when they had walked almost the full length of the train and were beginning to despair, they found one with two empty seats.

There was no room on the overhead racks for their bundles so they had to keep them on their knees. They had seats facing each other in the middle of the two rows. On one side of Nick sat a burly man, with a cap pulled down over his eyes, who seemed to be already asleep; on the other was an equally large woman with a basket on her knee from which was emanating the sound of a cat mewing. Nick felt squeezed between them but was pleased enough to have got on the train at all. No one was speaking.

The time for departure came and went. One or two other would-be passengers opened the door and tried to squash into the compartment but were immediately repulsed by the cat woman shouting, 'Full up! No room!' She had a piercing voice, one that stood a chance of being heard at the other end of the train. Nick grinned at Isabel, who was sitting between an elderly man and a nun wearing a wide wing-shaped bonnet.

Nick was happy to have Isabel with him. 'Of course I'm going to come with you!' she had said and flicked her hair back, in that decisive way she had. Eugenia had said Isabel was a girl who knew her own mind and so she was a girl after her own heart.

They had found the parting with Eugenia and Salvador difficult. In just over twenty-four hours they had become firm friends.

'We'll see you again,' Salvador had said. 'When life becomes a bit easier.'

Surely it must at some point, thought Nick, as they sat, tense, in the hot, stuffy, immobile train, waiting for something to happen. Surely people could not go on living under such conditions forever, fearing the police and the Civil Guard, fearing knocks on the door at night, worried about every step they took, every word they uttered. Salvador said wounds were much too raw yet for things to settle down. It could take a long time.

'Papers, get them ready!' a voice barked further along the corridor.

The passengers awoke from their apathy. Their hands curled tightly round their papers, their eyes slid from side to side.

Nick kept his eyes averted from Isabel. Exchanged looks are sometimes surmised to be guilty looks, Salvador had warned them. Nick kept his hand on the papers in his pocket, telling himself to keep cool, calm and collected – his mother's advice whenever he had an exam at school – and to try not to sweat. Guilty people sweated, so it was said. But then so did those who were nervous and not guilty. All the passengers in the compartment had their papers ready except for Nick's neighbour, who was snoring, with his chin dropped on to his chest.

The door slid back and a policeman stood in the opening. Everyone, apart from Nick's left-hand neighbour, immediately drew in their legs to give him a clear passage. The policeman rapped the sleeper on the side of the head with his knuckles.

'Wake up, dunderhead!'

The man, in his fright, almost toppled on to the floor.

'All right, out you get!'

The man, recovering his wits, and seeing the others holding their papers, spluttered 'But I have mine here.'

'Out, I said!' The policeman took him by the collar, whirled him round and kicked him out of the compartment. He went sprawling into the corridor.

No one else said a word.

'Right, Captain!' The policeman signalled to someone who had been waiting in the corridor. A man in a khaki uniform came into view. 'Come in, please, sir! I apologise that there are no first-class carriages on this train.'

'I am travelling purely out of emergency,' said the captain haughtily. 'My staff car broke down and I have to be in Seville tomorrow.'

'Tomorrow evening, I hope, sir. I fear the train will not make it before nightfall.'

'Nightfall!' The captain snorted and pursed his lips as if considering alternatives and finding none. Then he stepped into the compartment and the rest of the passengers pulled in their knees to make room.

'Move up, move up!' commanded the policeman. 'Let the captain have a seat by the window.'

They shuffled along and the soldier took the evicted man's seat after giving it a look of distaste. His knee-length mahogany-coloured boots gleamed. On his flat-crowned, peaked hat he wore three gold stars, and another three on a bar above his left pocket.

'A more deserving traveller,' said the policeman, nodding in the direction of the new arrival and defying anyone to challenge him, even by a glance. He then got round to examining their papers, which he studied with a fixed frown as if he were suspicious of each and every one of them.

'Your name?' he demanded of Isabel.

'Claudia Rosso,' she said in a calm, clear voice.

'You live in Borges, I see.'

'Yes.'

'And what is your purpose in travelling to Seville?'

'I am on my way to Málaga to visit my grandparents.'

'You are travelling alone?'

'No, with my brother.' Isabel indicated Nick on the other side and the policeman turned to look at him.

When he came to the nun, he merely nodded and said, 'God speed, Sister.'

Nick drew in a few deep silent breaths, trying to control the rapid beating of his heart. He hoped he would be able to answer as calmly as Isabel. What would the penalty be for travelling with forged papers? Never mind having entered the country illegally? Years in prison, probably. He did not let his mind linger on that.

Then it was his turn.

'So Rinaldo Rosso, you, too, live in Borges? With your parents?'

'Yes.'

'I see you are eighteen years old. Did you fight for our glorious leader, Franco?'

Nick nodded. Even in his nervousness he could not help reflecting that no one in Scotland would ever use such flowery language. The army officer was looking interested and had turned in his seat to address Nick.

'Where did you fight, lad?'

'Teruel.'

'Ah, I, too. Were you on the Heights?'

Nick nodded again. He said, aware of the croak in his voice, 'I was wounded there and sent home.'

'Badly injured, then, I take it?'

'Yes.'

What if they were to ask to see evidence of his wounds? Salvador had told him to say he'd suffered head injuries, concussion, internal bleeding. His injured, bandaged hand would not be sufficient for him to have been invalided out though he was deliberately sitting with it displayed on top of his pack.

The policeman handed the papers back to Nick. He wished the army officer a good journey, then left their compartment and carried on to the next one. The captain, however, had not lost interest in Nick.

'Whose command were you under? Was it General Aranda?'

Nick gave yet another nod. It seemed the safest response.

'Fine man. Fine soldier. We had the Republicans on the run, you remember, and then those blasted Internationals came in. Bloody cheek, British, French, Americans, interfering in our war. But we got back at them! We taught them a lesson finally. We estimated that we knocked off some fifteen thousand Reds in that exercise. Oh yes! Pretty good, eh?' The officer looked round the compartment but there was no response. 'And we must have taken around six or seven thousand prisoners. It's what I would call a most decisive and glorious victory!'

He went on to talk about his own glorious part in the battle, which was obviously all that he wanted to do. He was not really interested in Nick, who was required only to murmur now and then to show that he was listening. He was, in fact, listening attentively, thinking that this might be information he could use in future.

When there was a lull in their conversation the nun struck up one with Isabel.

'So you are going to visit your grandparents in Málaga, dear? That is a good thing for you to do. They're elderly, are they?'

'Yes.'

'Where is it that they live in Málaga? I know the city a little. My sister lives there.'

Isabel reeled off the address. The nun repeated the name of the street as if it might be familiar to her. 'That's near the market, isn't it?'

'Quite near,' agreed Isabel. 'Though it's a while since we visited them, so I don't really remember the city very clearly. During the war we couldn't go, of course.'

'But now we have peace, praise be to God. And God bless our dear leader.'

'Amen to that,' said the captain.

The nun was not finished yet, though, with her questions. She was in a chatty mood. Which church in Borges did Isabel's family worship at? Where had they been christened? Isabel struggled valiantly, managing to find some kind of answer for each question. Nick wondered if there was a Church of Santa María in Borges. Or had Isabel made it up? It was a good enough bet, anyway. There must be thousands of churches dedicated to the Virgin Mary in Spain. The more the nun carried on the more Isabel struggled. Nick thought how true it was that when first we practise to deceive what a tangled web we weave! Wasn't it Sir Walter Scott who had said that? He remembered his English teacher at school repeating it, relishing it, making it sound loaded, as if he suspected each and every one of them of deception and was warning them that they would not get away with it. That life seemed long ago.

The rest of the passengers, having nothing else to do, were listening to every word that Isabel and her neighbour were exchanging. Nick thought the captain was paying too much attention to Isabel. Perhaps he was thinking she was pretty. Nick did not like that idea but it would be safer if the man were thinking that than she might be an impostor.

The train left more than an hour and a half late, by which time everyone was dead tired and ready to sleep. It was a relief to hear the engine snorting and hissing into life and to smell the smoke. The train shuddered and lurched forwards to begin its long, tedious, jolting journey. Black smuts drifted in through the open window, but everyone tacitly agreed that it was much too hot to consider closing it.

Nick and Isabel met each other's eyes briefly and they gave a small nod as if to say, so far, so good, while acknowledging that it was only by the skin of their teeth that they were surviving. Nick was not sure that he wouldn't have preferred to risk a lift in a lorry. There would always be the chance of jumping off and making an escape. Here, they were trapped. And he had noticed that the captain was carrying a pistol.

Nick dozed intermittently, waking every now and then to see the darkness rushing past outside. Not that they were travelling fast. At times the train slowed to walking pace. The track was obviously in very poor repair, judging from the bumps and the jolts. Once or twice they thought they were about to be derailed. Only occasionally could a light be seen out in the *campo*. The sound of snoring and grunting within the compartment mingled with the rattle of the wheels beneath them. The cat, though, appeared to have subsided into silence. From time to time one of the passengers struggled up and, opening the door, disappeared along the corridor. When Nick himself went along, he found the toilet in a stinking state and overflowing.

A grey dawn broke and the passengers awoke feeling overheated and in ill humour. They scratched and yawned and their sour breath filled the compartment. The captain smoked a cigar, adding to the fug. He had given up pretending not to be affected by the heat and had removed his jacket. Nick saw that he had damp half-circles under his arms like everybody else and his forehead glistened with sweat.

They chugged on throughout the day. The minutes crawled. People dozed and grumbled. About the hardness of the seats and the slowness of the train. They finished their food and drained the last drops of water from their bottles. They ran their dry tongues over their parched lips. At intervals the train stopped altogether, as if needing a rest. Whenever it did, the passengers tumbled out to take the air and stretch their legs. The army captain stood apart, smoking yet another cigar. Walking beside the track Nick was better able to see the countryside than when travelling in the train with its small windows. The landscape had changed from the flat tableland of La Mancha, Don Quixote country, with windmills breaking the monotony every now and then, to become more undulating. As it grew dark Nick began to imagine the high sierras of Andalusia with their jagged peaks and red rocks, and the little white villages perched on high like splashes of snow, with groves of orange and lemon trees, olives, vines and avocados on the lower slopes. He could sense their smells. He could feel himself drawing closer to his father's country, and to his father.

They entered Seville at midnight.

Twenty

'I pray that you will find your grandparents in good health, dear,' the nun said to Isabel as they were approaching the station. 'I myself am travelling on to Málaga tomorrow morning. If you should need any help while you are there, come and ask for me at the Church of Los Santos Mártires. My name is Sister Encarnata.'

The Church of the Holy Martyrs. Nick wondered how many martyrs Spain had produced during its Civil War.

'You will find the church a little to the north of the market and not far from the river. Anyone will be able to tell you if you ask.'

'Thank you, Sister,' said Isabel.

'I shall be staying with my sister who lives nearby. Her name is Doña Rosalía Molina.'

The passengers were up on their feet, dragging their cases from the racks. In its basket, which now stank, the cat was complaining loudly and scrabbling at the wicker.

'She's been cooped up long enough,' said her owner.

That was how they all felt. It had been a long slow ride and the air in the compartment had become progressively heavier and staler as the day had worn on.

Finally the train lurched into the station and juddered to a violent stop, throwing the passengers off balance. They sprawled on top of each other and struggled to refind their feet. Nick held Isabel in his arms for a moment and for that brief passage of time they looked at each other and forgot that the rest of the passengers existed. Then they separated. Nick saw the nun giving them a strange look. But perhaps he had started to read too much into people's glances.

The captain brushed down his uniform with the tips of his fingers and looked displeased that he had been forced to have contact with another human being. He examined his boots, both back and front. He wrinkled his nose. The cat woman moaned.

'Every bone in my body will have been broken by the time we get off this contraption,' she declared.

'Give the General a little time and our country will be transformed,' said the captain. 'The infrastructure suffered atrociously under the Republicans. Everything went to rack and ruin. In future, our trains will run on time.'

That was what Italy's Fascist dictator, Mussolini, had promised his country. Nick remembered his mother commenting on it. 'What an idiot!' she had said. 'As if that is important in the scheme of things.'

They filed out, holding back to let the officer go first. The passengers in the corridor, many of whom had spent the night and the day there, flattened themselves against the wall to let him pass. He swung himself down off the step and went striding off. Soon the other travellers were following, hurrying towards the exit.

Sister Encarnata stopped to speak to Isabel and Nick, to tell them that trains for Málaga did not leave from this station. 'You have to go to Cádiz Station. I am spending the night in a convent. I hope to see you in the morning.' Then she, too, was gone.

The station soon had emptied, the lights dimmed. Looking about for somewhere to hole up, they found a pile of old sacks and boxes heaped in a corner. They had only just crawled inside when the first of the Civil Guard patrols came past. They spent the night in their uncomfortable hideaway, dozing intermittently, and at first light got up, feeling stiff and a little sore. The first thing Nick saw was a photograph of Franco staring out at him from a wall. He turned his eyes away.

When they emerged into the street they realised they were close to the river.

'It must be the Guadalquivir,' said Isabel. 'It's strange to see something that you've known only as a squiggle on a map.' She had travelled little in her country. Few people from her village had.

They stopped a street sweeper, who told them that Cádiz Station was on the other side of the city. He pointed northwards with the bundle of sticks that served as a brush. 'There's no direct route. You'll have to zigzag through the streets. You'll pass the cathedral. You can't miss that.'

As they walked they soon saw that Seville showed signs of destruction just as Madrid had, with ruined houses and burnt-out churches commonplace. Even so it was obvious that it must once have been a fine city and could be again.

They passed the cathedral with the tall bell tower alongside it. Nick recognised it and remembered going there with his father when he was small. They'd had a good day together, a happy day. They had climbed to the top of the tower and looked out over the rooftops. One day, when Seville's ruins had been swept away, he would come and climb the tower again with his father, and maybe with Isabel.

Sister Encarnata was already at the station and bustled up to meet them. 'They say there should be a train to Málaga at nine o'clock. It might take a miracle for it to leave at nine!' Her eyes twinkled.

It was almost eleven before it appeared and like the train from Madrid it was packed from end to end. This time, though, the journey did not last as long. Three hours later, after various stops and starts, they arrived in Málaga.

The nun fell into step beside Isabel and Nick on the platform. 'Can I help you find your way?'

'It's all right, thank you, I think we can manage,' said Nick, but the nun had taken Isabel's arm and was keeping pace with them. She accompanied them out into the street.

'What a waste.' Sister Encarnata sighed and shook her head at the devastation in the streets.

'It was the Italians who bombed the city, wasn't it?' said Nick. 'In support of Franco.'

'Well, that may be,' said Sister Encarnata uncertainly. 'Though I believe the Republicans did some burning of their own, early on.'

Nick felt Isabel press his arm. Yes, he should be careful. But when you were angry it was difficult to be careful.

'What was your grandparents' address again, dear?' asked Sister Encarnata.

Reluctantly Isabel repeated the false address that had been given to them by Salvador.

'Right, come with me! It's near the river and the market, if I recall correctly.'

They went, it being easier to do than to refuse, especially while the nun was holding on to Isabel. When they reached the street they saw that one end had sagged into a jagged, dusty heap. Further along windows were boarded up and dogs prowled.

'What number was it, dear?'

'Six.'

Six no longer existed, which for them was a piece of luck.

'You poor children, how distressing this must be for you! We must try to find out if anyone has any knowledge of your grandparents. We might ask at the Church of San Juan.'

'No, no,' protested Isabel, 'please don't trouble yourself further, Sister. We will make some enquiries.'

'But I can't leave you like this! Two poor children in a strange city.'

'We have relatives who live up in the mountains,' put in Nick. 'We could go there.' Somewhere in the sierras lived a cousin of his father and his family, though he could not remember the name of the village or where it was exactly. He had visited them only once, many years ago, when he was small.

Sister Encarnata was ignoring their protests. Spying a priest on the opposite side of the road, she went charging across to intercept him, her white, winged head-dress bobbing from side to side, her black skirt swirling over her bare, sandalled feet. An oncoming truck had to brake, but she did not appear to notice. 'Father Geronimo!' she cried, waving her arm. Glancing back at her charges, she said, 'He's an old friend! A good friend. He will help. Come along!'

Isabel turned to Nick and he held up his hands in surrender. They followed Sister Encarnata across the road. The priest, however, looked ancient and proved to be deaf.

'What are your grandparents' names?' asked Sister Encarnata.

'Juan and Sofía Rosso,' mumbled Isabel.

'JUAN AND SOFIA ROSSO,' bellowed the nun into the priest's ear. 'DO YOU KNOW THEM?'

He looked puzzled. 'I have a sister called Sofía.'

'ROSSO,' repeated Sister Encarnata, turning up the volume of her voice even more. Passers-by were giving them too much attention. 'THEY LIVED IN THIS PARISH.'

'You have worked in my parish, Sister?'

She shook her head. 'He is not the man he used to be,' she said to her two young companions.

A woman stopped. 'Were you asking about the Rossos? I used to know a family called Rosso.'

'Would you happen to know their given names?' asked Sister Encarnata.

Nick and Isabel edged back a step or two, anxious to make their escape before they attracted any more

130

attention. The situation was getting out of control. A couple of other women and an elderly man with a dog had paused on the edge of their group to listen. Any moment now a Civil Guard or a policeman might come by and stop to ask what was going on.

'The man was called Emilio. And his wife Josefa. But they disappeared. Well, you know how it is.' The woman dropped her voice, then looked over her shoulder.

'They are not our Rossos,' declared Sister Encarnata. 'Unless of course they might be related to your grandparents?' She appealed to Isabel. 'Could that be a possibility?'

'Please don't trouble yourself further,' said Nick firmly. 'We will go and look for our other relatives. But thank you very much for your help. You have been very kind.'

And with that he took Isabel by the arm and guided her back across the street. They walked swiftly, turned down a side street and kept on going until they felt confident that they had lost Sister Encarnata.

'She meant well,' said Isabel.

'I know. But unfortunately—' Nick shrugged. Unfortunately they couldn't come clean with anyone and tell the truth, not unless it was someone in the network of names given to him by Jean-Luc. They must now try to track down Carlos Cortes.

'How are we going to find his street?' asked Isabel.

They had quickly realised that a bombed city was difficult to navigate. Sometimes it was not possible to tell where one street ended and another began. Many street names had disappeared. Here and there blocks of houses existed intact as if by a miracle. Children played in among heaps of stone and tangled wires and broken, half-burnt furniture. In some places workmen had begun the task of clearing up. Dust hung thick in the air. And everywhere they looked there seemed to be beggars, with missing limbs, hirpling on make-shift crutches, wearing dirty

131

bandages wrapped round their heads or patches over empty eye sockets. They passed a gypsy woman sitting on the pavement with her baby. The woman's arms and legs were as thin as sticks, the baby looked half dead. When she saw them approaching she held out her cupped hand, but as they drew level and she registered that they were dishevelled and shabby-looking themselves, she dropped it.

'I wish we had some food to give them,' said Isabel in a cracked voice. 'They're starving.'

But they had nothing and what little money they had they must keep to see them through their journey.

They came to a small food shop and, pushing aside the beaded curtain, they entered, finding themselves in a dim poky room. There was nothing much on the counter, though a woman with a basket was negotiating the sale of some eggs. They stood back and waited. The shopkeeper eventually beat the woman down to his price.

'Oh, all right,' she said, with an air of resignation. She counted out her eggs into the box on the counter, her fingers curling round each one as if she was reluctant to let it go. 'You drive a hard bargain.' She looked weary. Her feet, in their rope sandals, were black and her dress torn. 'I have walked three hours from my village up in the hills to get here. I left at first light. Now I have to walk three hours back. I have had to leave my children alone all day.'

The shopkeeper shrugged. 'Such is life. It is hard for all of us. I do not find it easy to make a living either.' He removed the eggs from the counter in case she might take them back. He opened his till, took out a few coins and dropped them into her hand. She stared down at them.

'My children are starving. They have no father. Not any more.'

'Here is some bread for them, *señora*.' He produced a half-loaf from under the counter. 'Do not say I am ungenerous.'

She did not respond. She put the bread in her basket and shuffled out. Isabel stepped up to the counter and asked the man if he could help them with directions. He knew the street and told them how to get there. 'It's not far.'

Nick hesitated and then asked, 'Have you any food we could buy?' They had long since finished what Eugenia had given them.

'A bit of bread. I can't let you have any eggs. They are spoken for.' The man put a half-loaf on the counter, perhaps the other half of the one he had given the egg woman.

'Have you anything else at all?' asked Isabel.

'You have money?'

'Yes.'

He placed a tin of sardines on the counter and said the price, probably double what it should have been, but Isabel paid and they left the shop. They went round the corner and squatted on the pavement with their feet in the gutter. Nick twisted the key on the sardine tin and wound it back to reveal the tightly packed little silver fish sitting in their pool of olive oil. They tore off pieces of bread and ate them with the fish, soaking up the oil from the tin. They did not speak. The food tasted good. Nick offered Isabel his water-bottle and she drank, then he did, too.

Fortified, they set off to look for the street where Carlos Cortes lived. The southern sun was at its height, and it was hot, blisteringly hot. Wherever possible, they sought the shady side of the street. Nick longed for the refreshing winds that blew through his native glen. He thought of plunging into the loch and feeling its cool waters close over his back.

The shopkeeper had given them good directions. They arrived at the street within minutes to find that most of it was intact and people were still living there.

'Number thirty,' said Nick.

'It's still standing!' said Isabel. 'We seem to be in luck.'

'It's the first floor and the first flat on the right.'

They climbed the first flight of stairs. The doors were all blank and nameless. In front of the one on the right they stopped, and Nick knocked, giving three short and two long raps. They waited. There was a steady drip of water coming from somewhere.

Nick had to knock again. After the second time a voice spoke to them behind the door. 'Yes?'

'I'm looking for a friend.'

'What name?'

Nick felt uneasy, but then he always did at this point. And there was nothing else he could do but go through with it. He cleared his throat. 'I'm looking for Carlos Cortes.'

'He doesn't live here any more.'

'Since when?'

No answer.

'Do you know where he is now? Or where his mother is?'

There was still no answer.

The silence on the landing was feeling more and more eerie by the second. As they started to tiptoe away, one of the other doors on the landing opened, just a crack. They barely saw the person inside. It was a man, that was all they could make out.

'He was executed by the Nationalists,' said the man in a voice so low that they could only just make it out, 'along with some of the wounded in his ambulance.'

The door closed.

Nick ran down the stairs into the street and threw up his sardines and bread in the gutter.

Twenty one

'It doesn't necessarily mean your father was among them, Nick,' said Isabel.

'He was in Carlos's ambulance.'

'Yes, but Carlos might have got that batch to a first-aid station and taken on a new load.'

'Might.'

'Well, it's a *possibility*.'

She was just trying to be comforting, to find some ray of hope. He couldn't see it himself. He felt he'd reached the end of the line. And the end of his tether. He thought of poor Carlos Cortes driving his ambulance, taking the wounded away from the battlefield, taking his father, and then ending up . . . He should stop his thoughts before they developed into the worst scenario he could imagine, but they raced relentlessly on. His father taken prisoner along with Carlos and the other men, hauled out of the ambulance like a sack of potatoes, half dead already, propped up against a wall, and then the order to fire . . .

'Nicolás,' said Isabel softly, putting her hand over his, 'you've got to keep hoping.'

He was sweating badly. What a disgusting mess he was in. He must stink. He wished he could clean himself up. But there wouldn't be much chance of that. He felt his gorge rise. Was he going to be sick again? He felt sick, sick from the knowledge that his father might be, could well be, *dead*. And if he was dead he might never find where he had died or where he was buried. The country was full of mass graves.

'All right, Nicolás?' asked Isabel.

He gave a half-nod and turned back to look at the building they'd just left. He thought he caught a glimpse of a face at a window.

'Isabel, do you see a man up there at the window?'

She frowned. 'I can't see anyone.'

Nick looked again, saw no one, either. 'Maybe I was hallucinating.'

What were they to do now? For a start, they had to get out of the burning sun. Nick had the address of another contact in Málaga, one that had been given to him by Jean-Luc. They decided they might as well try it.

Wearily they set off again through the city streets. They were on the point of exhaustion, having spent one night on the train, and another on a station platform, and having slept little on either. The sun was dazzling, the heat blazing up from the pavements. Isabel had to ask the way several times. On one occasion, while she had gone to find someone, Nick thought he caught sight of a man dodging behind a blitzed house. He blinked, saw only rubble then. His head was playing him tricks. It must be the sun, though a few minutes before he'd had the feeling that they were being followed.

Isabel returned. 'Not far now. Five minutes' walk.'

They found the street but the house they were looking for no longer stood. It lay in a sad heap. Nick felt no surprise. And there seemed no point in asking anyone. It could be like opening up a new can of worms.

'We seem to have run out of luck,' he said.

'You don't look well, Nick. In fact, you look dreadful!'

He felt it. His head was thumping and his eyes couldn't seem to focus properly.

'You need water.' Isabel laid a hand against his forehead. 'You've got a temperature. You're bound to be dehydrated after being sick.'

'I'm just a drag on you.'

'Don't be silly!' She scrutinised the street, but there was no drinking well here like the one in her village. 'We need help.'

'Who's going to give it to us?'

'Sister Encarnata.'

'No, Isabel!'

'Why not?'

'It could be dangerous. The Church is on Franco's side, isn't it?'

'Officially it might be, that that doesn't mean all the nuns and priests take sides.'

'Francisco – one of the men who helped me up north – told me about a friend of his who was betrayed by a priest. They lived in the same village. They'd been neighbours. The man had known the priest since he was a boy.'

'These things happened in the war. And yes,' Isabel added quietly, 'they are still happening.'

'How can you be so calm about it?'

'Because I lived through it. If I'd had hysterics every time something terrible happened in our village I would be insane by now.'

Like her mother. Nick fell silent.

'I am not defending such things.'

'I know,' he muttered.

'I'm sure many of the clergy are neutral.'

'How can you be sure Sister Encarnata is? She was very keen to hang on to us.'

'She only wanted to be helpful. All right, I can't be absolutely sure. But my instinct tells me I can trust her. And there is no one else we can turn to.'

'Her sister could be married to an officer in the Civil Guard, for all we know. I'm sorry, Isabel, I didn't mean—' He broke off. He had not meant to suggest that anyone related to a member of the Civil Guard was not to be trusted, since it was obviously not true. He felt his head was about to split open like a tomato over-ripened in the sun.

'What other choice do we have?'

'We could go and look for my father's cousins. I'd rather be up in the mountains than in this hell of a city.' That was what it felt like, a hell on earth, with raging furnaces and desolation all around and people with missing limbs and desperate eyes.

'You don't even know where they live.'

'I sort of do.'

'What use is that? Aren't there dozens of little white villages up in the sierras? You said so yourself. We could wander for months and not find it.'

He tried to stand but the street tilted and the pavement came up to meet him, and he went down like a felled log. Isabel crouched beside him and put her hands under his armpits. 'Let me take your weight. Right, try to push up!' She hoisted him back on to his feet.

They staggered until they'd found their balance, then they stumbled on.

'You've done this before for me,' he muttered.

'Don't talk. Just save your energy.'

He could not think any more, he could barely see. He floundered along, seeing the street, the buildings, the people, pass in a blur. He heard Isabel's voice saying from time to time, 'Los Santos Mártires?' They came into a square.

'There should be a little street running off,' she said. 'Yes, here we are. There is even a sign for the church.'

They went up an alleyway, came into another square, smaller than the previous one, and there was the church, and it was open.

It was blessedly cool inside after the scorching heat of the streets. Isabel helped Nick on to a bench and went to find someone to ask about Sister Encarnata.

Candles were flickering, lighting up the gold on the altar and the niches at the sides of the church. There was a smell of incense and flowers. *Carnations*, thought Nick.

Their sharp smell was unmistakable. His mother grew them in her garden. And roses. She was fond of roses. Dark red velvety ones, others a soft yellow, some a vivid flaming orange. He closed his eyes and gave himself up to the silence.

He opened them when he became aware of someone sliding on to the bench beside him. His head jerked up.

'It's all right,' said the man, 'don't panic! Stay still. I'm a friend.'

Nick kept still. The man leant forwards and closed his eyes as if he were praying.

'Why did you want Carlos Cortes?'

'I was looking for someone.'

'Who?'

Nick hesitated.

'It's all right, I assure you. I truly am a friend.'

'Sebastián Torres.'

'He never came to Málaga. He was badly wounded.'

'I know that much.'

A man passed the end of their pew but he kept on going, up to the altar.

'They dropped him off with his relatives in Cómpeta before they got to Málaga.'

The man pressed Nick's hand and then rose.

'Thank you,' said Nick.

He took a look now at the man and felt sure that it was the person who had been following them and who had spoken to them from behind the door. He heard his footsteps retreat and fade and the church door close.

Nick must then either have dozed or passed out briefly, for he came round to hear two female voices buzzing about his head.

Can you stand up? Try. Lean on us. That's right, lad. Just a few steps . . .

A few steps, and the brilliant sun hit him in the eyes again.

'My sister lives just round the corner,' said Sister Encarnata.

Between them, Isabel and the nun supported him out of the church and across the square into a narrow street. They entered a building and climbed some stairs, and after that he was not sure what was happening. When he surfaced again he found he was lying on a bed and a woman in black was hovering near. And then came Sister Encarnata, bearing a basin of water. She started to sponge off his arms and legs with cool water while Isabel held a cup to his lips.

'Try to drink,' she urged.

He gagged.

'There's a little salt in it. You need salt.'

Each sip was an effort. His lips, his throat were parched, like sandpaper left out in the sun. For the next few hours he drifted in and out of consciousness, at times hearing voices that sounded garbled and made no sense at all.

He was delirious throughout the night, but in the morning he awoke with a clear head. The room no longer swam and tilted before his eyes. It was small, with white walls and covered half-way up with tiles in blue, green and yellow. They looked familiar. He thought his grandparents might have had similar tiles in their house in Nerja. They were common in Andalusia. The only furniture in the room, apart from the bed, was a wicker chair and a small table on which stood a glass half filled with water. On the opposite wall hung a large crucifix flanked by two religious pictures, one of Jesus on the cross, the other of his mother, Mary, in a sky-blue dress with a gold halo. Nick reached out his hand and lifted the glass and drank until he had drained it dry.

The door opened, and a woman put her head round. It was the woman in a black dress whom he had seen before. He was to learn that she was yet another war widow, though he never found out on which side her husband had fought. He did not want to know.

'I'm Doña Rosalía, Encarnata's sister. And how are you this morning, Rinaldo? Looking much better, I see.'

For a moment he thought she was speaking to someone else, then he remembered the name on his fake passport. 'I am, thank you,' he said.

'Would you like something to eat? I have a nice brown egg I can give you.' She had a cousin living in a village just outside Málaga who brought her a few eggs every week. 'I'm lucky. And I was early in the queue for the baker's and got a fresh loaf!'

She brought him a thick slice of the new bread, the egg lightly boiled and a cup of milk. She propped a pillow behind him. 'Now eat! You need to build your strength.' He smiled, remembering Marina, his first ministering angel.

There seemed to be no sign of Isabel. Had she gone? The fear that one morning he might wake to find she had disappeared had never been far from his mind. After all why would she want to stay with him? Everywhere he took her he led her into danger.

'Your sister has gone to church with Encarnata,' said Doña Rosalía. 'They should be back soon. She is such a lovely girl, Claudia. I would have liked to have had a daughter like her myself.'

Nick had just finished his breakfast when they returned. Isabel was wearing a black lace scarf over her hair. She came to him.

'It's wonderful to see you looking more like yourself. You've been doing a lot of raving in the night.'

'What was I saying?'

'All sorts of things. But you kept going on about somewhere called Cómpeta.'

Twenty two

On leaving the coast, the road to Cómpeta wound up into the mountains. For a while it would climb, then come down again, then go up, and all the time, on their left-hand side, there was a steep drop into the valley below. All around the mountains rose majestically and every now and then they spied a cluster of white houses perched high up, a remote village, reachable only by a precipitous track. Nick was amazed that people could live up there at all, so cut off from the world. The living must be poor.

They had been lucky and had got a lift with a neighbour of Doña Rosalía's as far as Caleta de Velez, a small fishing village. They had stayed a week in Doña Rosalía's flat, which had given Nick time to recover his strength fully. The nun's presence had made the house safe. No one was going to challenge her or come barging in with a search warrant. Neither Sister Encarnata nor Doña Rosalía had asked many questions. Nick and Isabel had told them they were planning to go and look for relatives living up in the hills, since they had not been able to find their grandparents. Apart from that, whatever the two women suspected, they knew nothing and would have nothing to report should they be questioned.

At midday, with the sun at its height, they stopped for lunch. Isabel laid out the bread, cheese and figs given to them by Doña Rosalía and two ripe oranges they'd picked up earlier from the ground. Eating their picnic in the shade of a small grove of old gnarled olive trees, they looked back at the wide blue panorama of the

Mediterranean Sea sparkling in the distance. It was so peaceful up here after war-torn Málaga. The grass was burnt brown by the sun but lavender, rosemary and thyme flourished, as did little deep-blue delphiniums and purple loosestrife. Before sitting down they had rubbed their hands with lavender sprigs to refresh them. Thistles abounded too, and ling heather, both of them reminding Nick of his native land. And there were prickly pears, with their thick plate-like prickly leaves shooting in all directions, the fruit ready for picking. There was no dust and no rubble. And it was quiet. The only sounds they could hear were the buzz of insects, the tinkle of goat bells somewhere near by, the noise of the wind.

Nick was relieved, too, to be in the open air again. Doña Rosalía had been more than kind, but after a week inside, going out only on short, nervous forays and accompanied always by the two women, he had felt cooped up like a bird in a cage, desperate to stretch his wings again.

'You're a country boy.' Isabel smiled at him.

'And you?'

'I don't know yet. Growing up in my little village I always dreamt of going to live in the city.'

'To Madrid?'

'I suppose. But it's in a mess now, isn't it? Everywhere is in Spain.' Her voice darkened.

'Not out here. It's beautiful up here. You can forget wars up here.'

The goat bells were coming closer and soon the herdsman came into sight over the crest of the hill, leading his little flock. There were about forty beasts in all, small and thin in the flank, as the herdsman himself was. His clothes hung almost in tatters and his face was burnt a dark mahogany by the sun. Nick remembered his father telling him that often the herds would walk all day, from dawn to dusk, seeking new pastures, covering many miles.

The herdsman greeted them; they responded and he stopped, though the goats continued to move about restlessly, nibbling grasses and shoots and rattling their bells.

'Going far?'

'Cómpeta.'

'That's my village. It's a good walk away.'

'We'll make it by nightfall, though?' asked Nick.

'Easily.' Then came the inevitable question. 'You know people there?'

'Yes.' Nick hesitated, but he thought that most people in this area would have supported the Republicans. 'The Torres family.'

'Gil Torres?'

Nick nodded.

'He is a relative?'

'A second cousin.'

'He's a good man.' The herdsman put his thumb and forefinger together and held them up. 'He's all right. A good journey to you both!'

The flock went on its way.

'He belonged to the right side, thank goodness,' said Nick, adding, on seeing the expression on Isabel's face, 'Now you couldn't say the Nationalists had *right* on their side. They were Fascists.'

'And the other side were Communists. Is one any better than the other?'

'They weren't all Communists. My dad was a Socialist. Anyway, Communism began because the poor and the workers had hardly any rights. No wonder the rich didn't like it when they lost the election to the Left. So they started up a revolution. They didn't want to lose their privileges.'

'It's not that simple. And not all Nationalists are rich.'

'But look at the people you had supporting you! Hitler and Mussolini. Hitler hates Jews. He wants to conquer Europe. He's already into Poland.'

'And you had Stalin. He's got plenty of blood on his hands. My father says he's out to conquer Europe *and* the rest of the world if he can get away with it.'

Their argument had become heated; they were glaring at each other. For a moment Nick hated Isabel for the fact that she had not been on the Republican side, his father's side, and he was appalled that he should feel this blind hate. He looked away from her, down into the valley where a donkey was plodding peacefully along with a load of straw on its back, a man in blue overalls walking behind, prodding it with a stick. Further on two oxen, roped together, were pulling a cart. The world moved slowly here. It was difficult to believe that war had ever troubled it.

How could Isabel *possibly* be for the Fascists and Franco?

She sighed. 'This is crazy, the two of us sitting up here in this beautiful place arguing about politics. Of course I don't approve of everything that went on. I hated all of it. I hate war! I hate people killing each other! But what was I to do? Stand in the street and shout, "Down with Franco!"? My father was in the Civil Guard, on Franco's side, don't forget.'

How could he forget? Her father's hands were stained with his blood; the marks on his back showed where the sergeant's booted feet had landed. But reason told Nick, now that he was cooling down, that Isabel could not be held responsible for anything her father had done, any more than he could for his. It was more than likely that his father would have blood on his hands too. Nick turned back to her. 'You're right. It's too good a day for quarrelling.' He drew her to him and kissed her.

They could not linger long, they must move on, even though the sun was high and it was siesta time for southerners. The going would be slow. They were wearing wide-brimmed straw hats provided by Doña

Rosalía, who had delivered them a lecture on the perils of sunstroke, an unnecessary lecture as far as Nick was concerned.

The little white village of Sayalonga appeared to be asleep as they passed by, apart from a barking dog that came snapping at their heels but did not follow them far. The narrow dusty road continued to twist and turn and climb higher and higher into the sierras. They saw a griffin vulture passing overhead and a great bustard. They were conscious of being in wild, remote country. A man on a donkey passed them going in the opposite direction and then another one leading a mule with panniers filled to the top with vegetables and, later, came a noisy motor bike travelling perilously close to the edge of the road. The verges were ragged and the drop to the valley below almost vertical. Even to look down made them feel dizzy.

After a while they were forced to take another break. They threw down their packs and slept for two hours in the shade of an overhanging rock, awaking in a stupor from the heat. They opened their eyes to find two men standing in front of them, feet astride, in a pose that suggested intimidation, with pistols tucked into the belts at their waist.

Nick and Isabel felt intimidated. They stayed where they were on the ground, making no move to get up, hardly daring to raise their eyes to look the men in the face. They were certainly not Civil Guard or police. Their trousers were baggy and creased and their boots scuffed and well worn. They must be outlaws, bandits who roamed the hills.

'What are you doing up here?' asked the taller of the two.

'We're on our way to Cómpeta,' said Nick, easing himself up into a sitting position where he felt a little less vulnerable.

'Cómpeta, eh? So what are you going there for?'

'To visit relatives.'

'And who would they be?'

Nick hesitated but thought it unlikely the men would be supporters of General Franco, any more than the goatherd had been. 'The Torres family.'

'Gil Torres?' The man sank down on to his haunches so that he was eye to eye with Nick. He had long hair and several days' growth of beard on his chin. He was a wild-looking character. 'I know Gil.'

'He's my father's cousin.'

'In that case . . .' The man extended a calloused hand and Nick took it. 'You are friends then. We will escort you to the edge of the village.'

The sun was dropping as they neared their destination, flooding the sierras with pink light, making Nick and Isabel catch their breath in wonder.

'There it is, that's Cómpeta,' said their long-haired guide, pointing at the opposite side of the valley, where a rash of white houses sprawled down the hillside, surrounded by vineyards.

They were ready to part, the men to go back into the hills, Nick and Isabel to move on and look for the Torres household.

'Tell Gil, Diego sends him his respects,' said their guide.

'And Silvestre,' added the other man.

They said their farewells and Nick and Isabel turned towards Cómpeta, their steps quickening as they reached the outskirts of the village. There were people about. Old men sat on benches, smoking, leaning on their sticks. A few younger ones lounged outside a bar. Women, some middle-aged, some elderly, many in black, strolled arm-in-arm, in pairs, deep in conversation. It was the time of day for the *paseo*, when the older members of the community left their houses to take the air. Later, the young ones would come out, girls linked together, boys walking separately. They might stop and exchange a bit of banter. It was the only chance they had of meeting. Courtships were carried on in this way. Nick was aware that in these villages the idea of him travelling alone with a girl would be strongly disapproved of, if it were known that they were not brother and sister.

In her village, said Isabel, no one went out on the *paseo* any more. People were too crushed to want to parade themselves in public. And some did not want to see their neighbours. The divisions and betrayals had been too great.

Nick recognised the steep street that led up to the main square. The Plaza de la Almijara. The name meant a place for drying out olives and perhaps it had been that originally, going back to the time when the Moors had ruled this part of Spain. Flowers hung from black wrought-iron balconies. War had not stopped the flowers growing.

They saw a small bar and approached a man standing at the door.

'Gil Torres?' he said. He turned and shouted into the bar behind him, 'Gil! Someone here looking for you.'

A moment later a greying, bearded man, tall for a southern Spaniard, emerged. He looked questioningly at the two strangers, then his gaze narrowed and he said to Nick, 'I think I know you, don't I?'

Nick nodded.

Gil Torres embraced him. 'You're his spitting image!'

'My father – is he—?'

Keeping an arm round Nick's shoulder, Gil said, 'Come home with me and I will tell you.'

Twenty three

The Torres family lived in a two-storeyed terraced house on an upper level of the village and consisted of Gil's wife Luisa, their daughter Carmen, who was thirteen, and their son, Antonio, who was seventeen, and tall, like his father. Luisa seemed a cheerful woman; she had a ready smile, though Nick thought there was something sad in her look. She was wearing black, which was not unusual for village women. His grandmother always had; she'd said it didn't show the dirt.

'You won't remember your cousin,' Gil said to his children, as he brought in the visitors. 'You were very young when he came to stay with us before. This is Nicolás, the son of my cousin Sebastián. And this is his friend Isabel.'

After much exclaiming and embracing of Nick, eyes were turned curiously on Isabel, who had stood back quietly during the family reunion.

'Isabel saved my life,' said Nick and she flushed, the colour showing even through the deep brown of her cheeks.

'Then we have much to be grateful to her for,' said Luisa, smiling at them both. 'You must have had a long hot walk to get here, so would you like to wash?'

'First,' said Nick, 'I want to know about my father. *Please!*'

'Of course,' said Gil.

'He was here, wasn't he? I was told so in Málaga.'

'Yes, he was brought here by his friend Carlos, an ambulance driver.'

Poor, poor Carlos, Nick thought again, with a knot in his throat. At this moment he could not bear to tell them what had happened to this brave man who had risked his life to bring his father up here into the mountains, and in the end had lost it.

'He was in a very bad way, your father,' said Gil.

'Is he—?' Nick took a deep breath. 'Is he dead?'

'We don't know.'

'You don't *know*?'

'He stayed with us for a few days and then Antonio and I took him down to the coast on a donkey. We left him at a friend's house in Nerja, someone he'd known since he was a boy and could trust totally. He was desperate to try to get back to Scotland. He thought if he could get to the coast, then maybe—' Gil shrugged. 'Maybe it will have been possible. But the coast is closely watched, the guards are everywhere. They skulk about, like rats ready for the kill. But who knows? Some do manage to get away. The trouble for your father was that he was too weak to make it on his own.'

Nick remembered the men up in the hills and told how they'd been kind enough to guide Isabel and himself down to Cómpeta. 'Diego and Silvestre send their respects. Are they bandits?'

'Bandits?' said Gil. 'No, not them. They're anti-Franco guerrillas. There are a number of them round here. They operate mostly at night. They are known as *niños de la noche*, even though they are no longer children.' Children of the night.

'Gil,' said his wife, 'you must tell Nick about his grandparents.'

'Are they dead?' asked Nick quickly.

'I'm afraid they are. Your grandfather caught flu early on in the war and it turned to pneumonia. Then your grandmother became ill. I fear, too, they were short of food, with your grandfather no longer being able to fish.

I managed to visit them once or twice but it wasn't easy to get into Nerja without being challenged by the guards. I was shocked when I saw them. I took some food but that wouldn't have lasted long.'

Nick was saddened but not surprised by the news. He had sensed that his grandparents might no longer be alive.

Luisa now urged the visitors to wash and refresh themselves. 'You will feel better for it. And then we shall eat.'

They washed out in the courtyard and put on clean clothes lent to them by Luisa and Antonio.

'We are about the same size, Nick, which is fortunate,' said Antonio. 'I am pleased to get to know my Scottish cousin.' He had an infectious smile, like his mother. Nick remembered them as a warm family, full of talk and laughter. The war may have subdued the laughter but the warmth was still there.

They settled round the table in the kitchen and Luisa dished out steaming platefuls of bean and goat stew. The meat was rather tough and needed much chewing, but no one would complain of that. Food was food. With it they drank some of the village wine, made from sweet muscatel grapes grown on the slopes. The family had a smallholding outside the village, on which they grew grapes, avocados, olives and oranges, and kept a pig and, of course, some goats. Their goats, half a dozen in number, were walked during the day by the herdsman they had met earlier. In addition, to add to their income, Torres, father and son, worked as stonemasons.

'You take work where you can get it,' said Gil, topping up their glasses.

They talked a little about the war to begin with, but only a little, the family presuming that Isabel was for the Republicans like themselves. She was quiet again during this talk. Nick would not dare to tell them that her father was a member of the Civil Guard.

The wine was potent and as the evening wore on the laughter began to bubble. It was good to be able to laugh. Antonio was marvellous at telling stories. About the man who lost his pig and found it lying fast asleep on his bed, snoring. Or the old woman who thought Antonio was a ghost when a bucket of whitewash had toppled on his head and he'd met her in the street after dark. She'd gone screaming into her house. 'My own fault,' he said ruefully. 'I had left the bucket badly balanced on top of a wall.' He was expressive with his gestures and had a fluency with words and a natural charm. No doubt he exaggerated, but he did it amusingly. Nick saw Isabel watching him while he talked, her face alight, and he had to look away.

She also listened closely when Antonio took up his guitar and played. Nick could play too; his father had taught him. Any Andalusian boy worth his salt should be able to play the guitar, his father had said. Nick was taken by surprise, though, when Luisa stood up suddenly, clasped her hands in front of her and, with a far-off look in her eyes, began to sing. She sang a plaintive flamenco song that spoke of grief and longing for a loved one who is gone. The expression on her face was so intense that Nick, even though he was used to such singing, found it almost too painful to look at her. When she sat down her husband said, '*Bravo*,' quietly and touched her hand.

They stayed late round the table until Luisa said, 'I think our guests need to sleep. I can see them beginning to droop. Like flowers deprived of water.' She smiled.

It was long past midnight and not even Carmen had gone to bed. She seemed as lively as ever. Spaniards like to go to bed late, Nick knew. It was the one area in which his father and mother did not agree, for she liked to go to bed early.

Isabel shared Carmen's room, and Nick, Antonio's.

'Perhaps one day I will come and visit you in Scotland,' said Antonio.

'I hope you will,' said Nick, struggling to stay awake, since it seemed that his cousin wanted to talk. 'But there might be war in Europe first. Before I left people were talking about it. They said it might be the only way to stop Hitler.'

'Don't let's talk about wars! We've had enough of that. Let's talk about nice things. Girls. Your Isabel has very lovely eyes. She seems a nice girl?'

'She is.'

'She must think a lot of you to leave her family and come away with you?'

'I don't know.'

'You don't know? Isn't she your *novia*?' Your fiancée.

'We're not engaged.'

'You're not? I'm surprised then that she would compromise herself in this way. She doesn't look that type of girl.'

'She's a wonderful girl . . .'

'You will have to marry her then.'

Nick did not reply. He went to sleep.

They were to set off early in the morning in spite of their late night. In the heat of mid-summer it was necessary to take advantage of the cooler hours. Yesterday had taxed them to their limits.

The whole family was up to see them on their way. Gil took Nick aside.

'Don't be too hopeful, lad. I didn't think your father could last long.'

At the moment Nick was feeling nothing, thinking nothing. A numbness had overtaken him. He only knew that he had to plod along until he came to the end of the trail. It was nearing its end. Once they reached the coast there would be nowhere else to go, except back to France, or to Scotland.

153

'I'm glad you all survived the war, at least,' he said.

'Not all of us,' said Gil quietly. 'Don't you recall we had another son? Our eldest, Luis. He would have been twenty next week.'

'I'm sorry!' Nick had forgotten but now remembered a boy, older than himself, a quiet boy who liked to read. He remembered, too, the song that Luisa had sung last night.

'We are not the only family to have suffered,' said Gil.

They shared a final embrace, holding on to each other for a few seconds, reluctant to let go.

'I'll be back, I promise,' said Nick. 'Sometime.' In those few brief hours he had felt the bonds of family renewed between them.

'You will always be welcome. You are one of us.' Nick had been told that before, by Francisco, early on in his journey. All the people who had helped him had made him feel 'one of them'. 'You remember the address I told you, of Jaime the fisherman?' asked Gil. 'Good. So for now, Nicolás, good luck! And try to let me know about your father.'

Isabel was kissed farewell by Gil and his wife and children in turn and told that she, too, would be welcome. 'We bless you for having saved Nicolás for us,' said Luisa.

Nick and Isabel made their way down the road, turning at the corner to wave, then they were on their own again.

'What nice people,' said Isabel.

'Antonio thought you were nice.'

'I thought he was, too.'

'Yes, you did, didn't you?'

Isabel glanced sharply at him and he looked away.

Before breakfast, he had been alone for a few minutes with Luisa in the kitchen. She had had a quiet word with him. 'Isabel is a delightful girl. We have taken her to our hearts already. You must look after her. I am sure you will treat her honourably, especially since it is quite unusual

154

for two young people like yourselves to be travelling in this way. Once it is known that she has been with you, no other man will take her.'

Isabel was moving ahead with her long easy stride. He wondered if he would ever be able to take her walking with him on the Scottish hills.

They did not say much for a while. Ahead lay another long day's walk but, at least, this time, they were going mostly downhill, which was easier on the legs and lungs. Their route today lay to the east of the one they had taken yesterday, though the terrain was much the same. By the time they stopped for lunch and a siesta, they had made considerable progress. Not far below them lay the white buildings of Torrox, another Moorish village, and beyond that, the blue, glittering sea, their goal.

They reached it in the late afternoon. They approached it cautiously, but once they'd seen that there were no guards about they went right down on to the shore. The waves were gentle, making little frills of white along the edge of the sand as they rippled in. Out at sea lay a couple of small becalmed fishing boats. Isabel and Nick pulled off their outer clothes and plunged into the cool salty water. They frisked and frolicked about, ducking their heads below the surface and re-emerging, tossing their heads and laughing. Nick swam out a little way but came back in as soon as he realised that Isabel could not swim. Being brought up in a landlocked village kilometres from the sea, she would not have had the opportunity to learn.

She came out first and pulled her dress back over her head. Then she stretched out, letting the sun dry her. A few minutes later, Nick joined her.

'That was wonderful,' she said. 'I've often wondered what it would feel like, to be in the sea. Do you live far from the sea in Scotland?'

'Not far. Scotland's not very wide so you can get to the coast quite easily. But the sea's not as warm as this.'

Isabel sighed and sat up. 'I could stay here forever but I suppose we should get moving. We want to get to Nerja before dark, don't we?'

Her face glowed in the mellow rays of the early evening sun. Nick moved closer to her and kissed her.

'Do you remember what I told you way back?' Way back. How long ago was that? It seemed like a lifetime. Time had lost any definition for them in terms of days of the week or weeks of the month. They had lived from sunrise to sunset.

'That was before you knew me properly.' She smiled.

'I knew you well enough.' He kissed her again. 'I meant it. I mean it now.'

They had not noticed a fishing boat coming in until they were disturbed by men's voices. The boat bumped on to the shore and two fishermen jumped out to haul it up onto dry land.

'We'd better go,' said Nick.

They followed the coast round. It was going to be a magnificent sunset. The rapidly sinking sun was sending shafts of pink and red across the sea, whose own colour had bled away to a pale milky hue.

They were so taken by the sunset that they had forgotten to be watchful. They turned a corner and walked into the arms of two members of the Civil Guard. Each carried a rifle and had a pistol tucked into his belt.

'Papers!' came the immediate demand.

They produced them.

'You are strangers here, we see. What are you doing in Nerja?'

Nick had his answer ready. He said they had gone to Málaga to look for their grandparents and found that their apartment had been bombed. One of the neighbours had told them they had left the city and gone along the coast.

'You're sleeping rough, I suppose?'

Nick tacitly assented.

'Just stay away from the coast itself, understand? We have nightly patrols out. Anyone prowling about is liable to be shot.'

Nick nodded again. They were allowed to move on, but the encounter had made them nervous. They left the shore and completed their journey by road.

Nerja was another of the small fishing villages spread along the coast. The light was fading fast as they came into its narrow streets. Women gossiped on corners. Children in the usual ragged clothes played in the road. As in all these little settlements, whether on the coast or in the hills, life would be harsh and difficult. They were poor places. A fisherman on a corner was standing beside his paltry catch, a dozen or so small silver fish in a wooden box. Two women were haggling with him. He was saying he had to eat, as did his children. Dogs skulked close by, their mouths ready to snap on any fallen morsel.

Nick asked an elderly man, sitting on a chair outside his door, for directions.

Keep going, he told them, past the church and the Balcón. 'You can't miss it. Then take the first street angling round on the right.'

The Balcón was the Balcón de Europa, Balcony of Europe – a wide piece of land jutting out into the sea, resembling a balcony, and fringed with palm trees. People were out doing the *paseo*. Isabel and Nick took a little detour to join them, stopping at the Balcón's outer edge to admire the magnificent view. They turned to look back towards Málaga, where the sun was about to slide down into the water. They lingered, glad to be part of a crowd. Nick was at the stage of wanting to arrive quickly at the final address, yet wanting to hold off at the same time, apprehensive in case he might be greeted with bad news.

'Come on,' said Isabel, taking his hand and leading him away.

It was almost dark when they reached the street of Jaime the fisherman. Here and there a lamp glowed at a window. Isabel's hand tightened round Nick's.

They found Jaime's house easily: a low, one-storeyed dwelling, on the right-hand side of the street, the sea side. Its shutters were closed and no light showed. Nick knocked. They stood back, feeling the quietness of the street wrapping itself round them.

They were beginning to think no one was coming, when they heard shuffling at the back of the door. It opened a crack.

'Yes?'

Nick cleared his throat. 'I'm looking for Sebastián Torres.'

Silence.

'I am his son Nicolás, from Scotland.'

'Who is with you?'

'A friend. Isabel. We have just come from Cómpeta, from the house of Gil Torres, my father's cousin. He gave us your address.'

The door opened further. Nick's throat was bone dry.

'Is my father here?' he asked, his voice squeaking from the strain.

'He is,' said the man, and opened the door fully.

Twenty four

Nick was shaken by the sight of his father even though he had been forewarned. Sebastián Torres was a shadow of the man he had been three years before. He lay on a couch in a back room, his limbs stick-like, the hollows in his face accentuated by the dim lamplight. Nick squatted beside him, holding his hand.

'I am so happy to see you, son.' His father's eyes shone with tears. 'Last time I saw you you were a boy. Now you are grown into a man. A fine man, too, from what I see.'

'Father, I am going to take you home and we will get a good doctor to treat you.'

'I want you to take me home, if you can. I want it more than anything else! I want to see your mother again. As for the doctor who will make me better, I doubt it. I think I am "not long for this world".' He said the last part in English – they had been speaking Spanish. 'Isn't that what your Scottish grandmother would say? She used to announce it when her cheeks were full of colour and her eyes as bright as buttons. And we used to say she would see us all out!'

'You will get better, Dad! You've *got* to,' insisted Nick. He would bring his father through with the strength of his own body. He would transmit his energy to him.

'You were always stubborn, Nicolás.' His father smiled. 'You never did give in easily, even though at times you should have done! Now, tell me about your mother. And then how you got here. I want to know everything.'

They stayed for a long time, Nick talking, his father listening, putting in the occasional question.

'There are so many good people in the world,' sighed Sebastián, 'helping me, helping you. You have been passed from hand to hand by friends, people you will never forget. Jaime, my host here, my old friend, is a poor fisherman, but he's willing to share his last crumb with me. And to run the risk of having me here in his house.'

Nick told his father then about Isabel, who had stayed in the other room.

'Is my son in love? I think you blush. I must see this girl, if she is as wonderful as you tell me! Perhaps not now, though. In the morning. Tonight I want to think only about you and the new person you've become.'

'You're tired. I've tired you.'

'How could you do that? It's my body that tires me.'

Nick leant over and kissed his father, then he rose and left the room. Outside in the corridor he shed the tears that he had been holding back.

He felt a hand on his shoulder. 'It's all right,' said Isabel softly. 'It's good to cry.' He turned to her and let her put her arms round him.

When he had recovered they went through to the kitchen, where their host was cleaning his catch. The sparsely furnished room smelt strongly of fish. A bucket speckled with fish scales stood in the corner. The room was hot, too, from the charcoal-fuelled stove.

'Sit down,' said Jaime, 'and help yourself to some wine. Or water.' There were two flagons on the table. 'In a few minutes we shall eat.'

He put a pan on the stove, poured in some oil and then flung in the newly cleaned fish. They began to sizzle madly and within minutes were on their plates on the table.

'And, so, Nick,' asked Jaime, as he came to join them, 'what do you think of your father?'

'I'm worried. He's in bad shape.'

'I'm afraid you're right. He was badly wounded and on top of that he got dysentery. It was rife in the camps during the war. Nothing could stop it.' Jaime raised his arms in a shrug. 'I've done what I could for him but I couldn't fetch a doctor. It would have been too much of a risk. But I'm hoping to arrange a lift for him to Gibraltar in a friend's boat.'

'When?'

'Soon.'

'Can you make it as soon as possible?' asked Nick urgently. 'I must get him to a doctor.'

'I'll do my best.'

'From Gibraltar we should be able to get a boat to England!' Since Gibraltar belonged to Britain, British ships must call there.

'We will have a problem even getting him into a fishing boat. He can't walk more than a few steps. He's not really fit to travel.'

'But he's determined to.'

'Men can do many things when they are determined,' said Jaime.

'Women, too,' said Isabel with a little smile.

'That is true.' Nick returned her smile.

Later, when he and Jaime were washing out in the yard, Jaime asked him, 'The girl? Is she going too?'

'I'm not sure.'

'She can't stay here, you know.'

'Of course not.'

In the morning, his father put the same question and Nick gave the same answer, but adding, 'I am going to ask her.'

'She won't have a passport to travel.'

'Neither do we.'

'But we can tell the authorities that we have British passports back home.' Both Nick and his father had dual citizenship, British as well as Spanish. 'They'll no doubt check before they let us land to make sure we're not coming in illegally.'

'There'll be a way,' said Nick. 'They'll *have* to let her come. We can't leave her here.'

'She may not want to come, have you thought of that?'

Nick had, of course, thought of that, but he said nothing.

'I think I should like to meet her now, Nick.' His father's voice was weakening.

Nick went to fetch Isabel. She pulled up a chair to his father's bedside and they spoke a few words together, not too many. There was so much they could have said that it was difficult to talk about small things, as she said afterwards to Nick. Sebastián Torres thanked her for saving his son's life. She replied that it was nothing. He said that for him it meant everything.

They left him to doze. Soon afterwards, Jaime came in, fresh from the sea, dropping his rubber boots off in the vestibule. He had gone out about four when it was still dark and the stars were bright in the sky. Nick had wakened when Jaime got up and had gone out for a breath of fresh air. He had walked to the end of the garden and stood listening to the steady pounding of the waves below and watching the little yellow lights twinkling out at sea. Fishing boats most likely, though perhaps one could belong to a coast-guard patrol. The night scent of jasmine had reminded him of the little garden at the back of his grandparents' house and he had felt sad that he would never see them again.

'Everything's set up with my friend Miguel,' said Jaime now. 'He will take your father on board just after eleven o'clock tonight.'

'Tonight? So soon?' said Nick. 'But that's good.' He must talk to Isabel; he could not put it off any longer.

'It suits Miguel better. We have to get Sebastián along the street and down a flight of steps to the beach. The cliff is too steep here. Miguel will give us a signal to tell us whether the coast is clear.'

'You can trust him?'

'With my life.'

'What about when we're on the boat? The police patrol offshore, don't they?'

'Sebastián will lie in the bottom of the boat, covered with a tarpaulin. Miguel will be fishing, as normal, except that he is going to stray out of his usual waters. You will be his deck-hand. His boat is bigger than mine.'

Would there be room for Isabel? Nick supposed she could be passed off as a deck-hand if she were to wear trousers and hide her hair under a cap. It would be dark. She was listening with an impassive face, giving Nick no clue as to what she was thinking. He had to talk to her straight away. He asked Jaime if it would be all right if they went for a walk.

'Be careful, though. You don't want to mess up our plans now.'

'We've got papers. If we're stopped we have a story ready. And don't worry, we won't let anyone know where we're staying.'

'Go east along the beach, away from the village. You'll see a few fishermen but they won't bother you. They don't make trouble or talk to the guards.'

Jaime checked the street first and then Nick and Isabel slipped out. At the far end they took the steps leading down to the beach, Nick registering how steep they were and how difficult it would be to manoeuvre his father down them in the dark. This part of the village sat high above the sea.

They walked eastwards, as Jaime had suggested, clambering over rocky outcroppings to reach a wide, curving bay, protected by high cliffs on its landward side. Some fishing boats were drawn up on the shore and a handful of men sat mending their nets. They looked round at the couple as they passed, but no one called out a greeting.

The day, like those that had preceded it, was calm and cloudless. Nick and Isabel walked hand-in-hand at the edge of the sea, letting the waves break over their ankles. Ahead they could see no other human being. On their left rose the lofty sierras. It was difficult to imagine war raging in such a place, shattering its peace.

'Isabel,' said Nick, summoning up his courage, 'I must talk to you.'

'Must you?' Her voice sounded guarded.

'I want you to come with us to Scotland. Will you come?'

Twenty five

'How could I come to Scotland?' asked Isabel. 'I don't even speak your language.'

'You could learn. My father learnt after he met my mother.'

'I have no money. I have nothing to bring with me. No clothes even, except what I'm wearing.' She held out her arms. Her blue cotton dress was bleached from the sun and frayed around the hem.

'We can buy clothes for you.'

'What work could I do?'

'I would look after you. I would earn money.'

'How could you do that? You have to go back to school. You said you had another year before you finish.'

'I could leave. Get a job on a farm.'

'That's not what you want to do. You'd resent it after a while. You'd resent me.'

'No!'

'You want to go to university. You want to be a marine biologist, you've told me so. You said you wanted to be one ever since you were a small boy.'

'I may not be able to. There may be a war. In a year or so I would be old enough to be called up.'

'And what would I do if there was a war and you went away to fight? I would be left in a strange country, alone.'

'You'd have my mother.'

'I don't know her. Nick, don't you see, it's impossible?'

'It's not, Isabel, it's not! I love you, I really do.'

'Dear Nick, I love you too.'

They moved into each other's arms. Nick held her tightly. It was going to be all right now. She loved him, she had just said so.

'So you'll come?' he said.

She shook her head. She was crying. 'I can't. It wouldn't work. There would be too many problems.'

'You don't really love me, then?' He drew back.

'I do. But it is all too difficult, you've got to see that.'

He saw nothing but that he wanted her to come with him. 'Please, Isabel! I want to marry you. I don't care if we're too young. He set about trying to persuade her, to cajole her, but all the time she shook her head and cried. In the end he sat down on the sand and covered his face with his hands. She knelt beside him.

'After a while you'll see that everything I've said is true, Nick. You have to put your mind to getting your father back. That will take every bit of your energy. And there is no room for me in all of that. I would be an extra problem.'

He felt gutted of energy, like the fish that Jaime had slit up the middle to pull out their innards.

Isabel looked up and frowned. 'Nick, there's someone on top of the cliff watching us.'

Nick checked. 'You're right,' he said quietly. There always seemed to be someone watching. Danger was never far away. 'It's a guard.' He could tell by the tricorn hat outlined against the sky.

They got up and walked towards the shelter of the cliffs, resisting the impulse to run. Once underneath they would not be seen from above. Nick had noticed several cave-like niches in among the rocks further back. They retraced their steps until they found an opening and crawled inside. The roar of the waves slapping against the rocks drowned out all other sound; they would not hear anyone approaching. A few minutes later they saw a stout pair of booted legs go lumbering past their hiding place.

Nick reached for Isabel's hand. There would be no peace for them until they got away. Both of them. He was determined to take her with him.

When, finally, they decided to risk coming out, their arms and legs felt cramped and their knees were scraped from the rocks. There was no one about and they made it safely back to Jaime's. Nick went at once to see his father.

'You were a long time.' Sebastián raised an eyebrow questioningly. 'You talked to Isabel?'

'She says she can't come. But I've got to make her. I've *got* to.'

'You can't make people. You're asking her to do a big thing. To leave her country.'

'You left.'

'I was older. She is very young to take such a big decision.'

'But everything's so terrible here. I can't leave her behind. People are afraid of their own shadows!'

'We have to hope that will change, given time.'

'How much time? Isabel can't even go back to her family. Her father would kill her!'

'Because she went away with you?'

'Partly. But also because he's a sergeant in the Civil Guard.'

'Then, of course, she never could go home.'

Neither Nick nor Isabel had any appetite when it came time for the evening meal, but they ate everything on their plates, knowing that each fish was precious to Jaime. None of them spoke. Jaime was a man of few words anyway. When he got up to go and see if Sebastián wanted anything other than the bread and milk he'd requested, Nick put his hand over Isabel's where it lay on the table top.

'You can still change your mind. I want you to change your mind.'

'I know.' She didn't look up.

'What would you do if you stayed? You can't go home. Would you go to your aunt in Madrid? But how would you get there? You can't walk all that way. You can't go on your own.'

'Doña Rosalía said that I could come and live with her in Málaga. She would like that. She has never had a daughter.'

That chilled him. So she had discussed it with Doña Rosalía back then. 'What did you tell her?'

'That I would think about it.'

'And what are you thinking?'

'That I could live with her. She's a very kind person.'

'So you have made up your mind?'

Isabel did not answer.

Jaime returned, carrying an empty bowl. 'It's good that he's eaten something. I think, Nicolás, we had better start getting ready. Can you help your father to wash and change his shirt?'

Isabel got up to clear the dishes and wash them in a bowl outside in the yard. Nick went to his father. It took some time to help him wash and change. Each movement was painful for him. Nick saw the spasms contorting his father's face and wondered if it would be possible to get him all the way to Scotland.

Soon it was time to roll up his blanket and pack his haversack.

'Isabel?' He appealed to her for the last time.

'I'm going to say goodbye now,' she said. 'I couldn't bear to come and watch the boat taking you away from me.'

Twenty six

Nick stood on the deck of a tramp steamer *en route* from Marseilles to Algeciras on the south coast of Spain. It was the cheapest passage he had been able to find. He was enjoying the sea breeze. Even offshore it was hot. On land the temperatures must be climbing to over a hundred degrees. He remembered hot sweltering days in the high sierras, where there had been little respite from the gruelling sun. He remembered his relief when he'd reached Scotland and felt the cool air on his skin. Since then he had fought in the desert in immense heat and in the Italian mountains in intense cold.

He had spent most of the journey on deck, watching the Spanish coastline unfold. As they drew further south his binoculars were seldom from his eyes. His interest quickened when one of the deck-hands pointed across the water and said, 'That'll be Motril. That's Andalusia across there, my homeland.'

A series of small white fishing villages were coming up. Nick had a map of Spain with him. Almuñecar. Maro. Nerja. Was that one Nerja? He recognised the Balcón de Europa jutting out into the sea, remembered standing there with Isabel, gazing at the horizon, watching the sunset. He kept his gaze fastened on the straggly white line of buildings that comprised the village until they were left behind. What would Jaime the fisherman be doing now? Still fishing, probably. He might even be in one of the small fishing boats lying close to shore. He intended to visit Jaime and thank him properly for what he had done for his father. He thought, too, of Marina. She had asked him to send back word about his safety, which he had not been able to do. If he had sent a letter with a British stamp, the Spanish authorities would probably have opened it. He would write from Málaga, but he would phrase his letter carefully in order not to cause trouble for her or Dr Fuentes. He would also write to Salvador and Eugenia, and Francisco, the first person to take him in and give him shelter.

Now he looked beyond the coast, up to the sierras. Somewhere up there among those jagged peaks lived his cousins. His family. He hoped no harm would have come to them, that they would not have fallen foul of Franco's regime. From what he had heard that was still easy to do. He would visit them. He wanted to be reunited with them, to get to know them better. Carmen would be twenty years old now; she might even be married. Antonio would be twenty-four, one year older than him. He might also be married, but Nick put that thought out of his mind.

There was no doubting Málaga when it came into view. It was so much busier than any of the other settlements, a busy seaport with a fair-sized town behind it. A number of ships of varying size were docked in the port, commercial vessels mostly, tankers, coal boats, fishing trawlers. Church spires spiked the skyline. Among them was Los Santos Mártires. Nick thought of Sister Encarnata and Doña Rosalía and, of course, of Isabel.

They sailed on, passing Torremolinos, Fuengirola, Marbella, and other small villages, until they saw the Rock of Gibraltar ahead. The sight of it brought back vivid, emotional memories for Nick. Getting his father ashore from Miguel's rocking fishing boat. Carrying him up on to the rocks, leaving him to lie alone in the dark. Going to seek help, finding a lodging house where they could stay cheaply for a few days until he found a ship that would agree to take them, on the promise that their passage would be paid once they reached Southampton. He did not know how but, in the end, he had managed it all.

They were rounding the Rock, heading into the port of Algeciras. Across the Strait of Gibraltar lay Morocco. The distance between Spain and North Africa was narrow here. Soon he would be back on Spanish soil again. His heartbeat quickened. He put away his binoculars.

This time he was arriving legally in the country, carrying a British passport and a Spanish visa. He need not fear the Civil Guard, though he had been warned that it would be wise to be wary of them and avoid altercations, since Spain was a police state and Franco ruled as a dictator.

In his wallet he had enough pesetas to pay for his travel and board and lodging in modest *fondas*. He would not have to sleep rough. When he had been demobbed from the army the previous month he had been given a sum of money, to which his mother had added. 'Stay there as long as you like,' she had told him, 'stay as long as you need to. After all, you've waited seven years.' He had had no other choice but to wait, with the Second World War intervening.

When they docked, a customs official came on board. He examined Nick's passport and visa and handed them back with a curt nod. He was free to go ashore. Slinging his rucksack over one shoulder, he made his way down the unsteady gangplank, taking care not to jar his right knee. He had been wounded in Italy and as a result walked with a limp. His long excursions up into the Scottish hills were curtailed now, but he had not let his injury stop him completely.

The quays were bustling. Seamen, dockers, fish sellers, traders, swarmed about, shouting to each other at the top of their voices. Spaniards tended to be noisy, Nick remembered, though immediately after the Civil War, when he had last been there, they had been more muted. A swarm of young gypsy girls appeared suddenly, as if from nowhere, surrounding him so quickly that he had no time to turn round. One of the girls held a bunch of red roses aloft.

'Buy a rose, kind sir! *Guapo señor*!' Handsome sir!

Nick tried to push through. Hands tugged at his arms, fingers scratched his face.

'Buy a rose for your sweetheart!'

'No, thank you.'

'He has no sweetheart!' Their laughter burst around his head. He made his escape, with the girls following before they dropped back, having sighted a new target. He wiped his brow on the back of his arm. He did not intend to stay long in Algeciras. His father had always said it was a hectic place.

The bus to Málaga wound its jolting way around the coast, calling in at every tiny settlement. At times it stopped for a break and then Nick got out and walked by the sea or else he found a shack where he could buy a cold drink. They arrived at their destination as it was getting dark.

He had often arrived at destinations when the sun was dropping, entered strange streets under cover of darkness. He felt more relaxed now that he was no longer walking in the full light of day. A hangover perhaps from those previous times. The pink-stained western sky and the glittering of the lamps in the purple dusk were evocative and brought back memories that made his throat tighten. They brought back memories of a girl with long black hair walking with a smooth even stride.

The streets of Málaga had been cleared of the rubble that had once littered them. Rebuilding had taken place, though gaps remained. He passed two members of the

Civil Guard who gave him curious looks and he felt a little shiver run up his spine, even though he was now a legal visitor. Once the guards were out of earshot, he stopped a woman and asked her for directions to Los Santos Mártires. It was only a few minutes' walk, she said. He needed the few minutes to compose himself.

Now that he was here, he was wondering if he had been mad to come. He had not seen this girl – this young woman – for seven years, and had known her for no more than a month, an intense, emotional month it was true, but only for that short span of time. She might have left Málaga. She might be married. She might have married his cousin Antonio. She had liked Antonio and he had liked her. Hadn't she been charmed by his stories? Antonio had made her eyes light up. She might have gone up to Cómpeta to visit the family. Luisa had invited her to come back any time. And if she did still happen to be here in Málaga and free, what could he offer her? In October he would go to university to study marine biology on an ex-serviceman's grant. For the next four years he would have little money.

After his father's death he had talked to his mother about Isabel. She had said, 'The years I had with your father were good years and they will sustain me in the time ahead. I know you didn't have as long with Isabel, but you might come to feel the same when you look back. Sometimes people meet too young. The time is wrong. There was no way forwards at that point for the two of you, she was wise to see that.'

'She is wise.'

'But you know it yourself as well.'

His father died a week after arriving back at their home in the Highlands, but it was a relief for all of them that he was there. He was buried in the village churchyard, overlooking a loch on one side and hills on the other. It was what he had wanted.

Nick recognised the narrow alley. At the end of it he should come into the square where Los Santos Mártires was located. He did. He passed the church and went round the corner to Calle Comedias. He recognised the door, too. He tested it to see if it was locked and finding it open he went inside and climbed the stairs to the first floor.

Faced with the door to Doña Rosalía's apartment, and possibly to Isabel, he paused again. Should he knock, or not? He raised his hand, then dropped it. Isabel might have forgotten him. It was still not too late to change his mind, to listen to the common sense in his head telling him that he should have left well alone. But it was not well, not for him, at any rate. He had had to come because he had unfinished business and until it was finished one way or the other he would not be able to get on with the next part of his life. While he was in the army, caught up in the war, everything had been put on hold.

He knocked, waited, listened. How many doors had he once stood in front of, waiting to see if anyone would come, his nerves jangling in case the person who opened the door would prove to be an enemy?

No one came. He knocked again, more insistently. But still no one came. Perhaps they had moved away. Or Doña Rosalía might have died. He knocked again and again until finally he turned away, dejected.

He returned to the square and after a moment's pause entered the church. Immediately he became aware of a powerful smell of lilies. He stood still. In front of the altar two women were arranging flowers. One was elderly, the other young. Nick felt himself begin to tremble.

The women, aware that someone had entered, glanced round. For a moment neither moved, then the younger of the two detached herself and came slowly down the aisle. She stopped before she reached him. She was wearing a red silk scarf over her head.

'Nick,' she said.

'Isabel.'

They looked at each other and each saw that the other had changed in the seven years. Nick felt suddenly shy and realised that Isabel did too. But realised also that everything about her was familiar. He knew that strong-boned face and those dark eyes and the way she held herself so straight and tall. She was not a stranger. He put out his hand and without hesitation she took it. As they left the church she let the scarf slip from her head and her long dark hair swung free.

'I'm glad you haven't cut your hair,' he said.

She smiled, then, noticing his limp, she frowned. 'What's happened to your leg?' He told her. 'I wondered if you might have been in the war,' she said.

'So you did think about me?'

'Of course! You have a lot to tell me, Nick.'

'And you me.'

They walked down through the town to the waterfront. The night air was balmy and warm. They sat on a wall and watched the lights on the moored boats bobbing gently in the swell. A full moon was casting its silvery light over the dark water making it shimmer and shine. When Nick slipped his arm round Isabel's waist, she let it lie.

'You first, Nick. I want to hear about your father.' After learning that he had died, she said, 'Jaime and I didn't think he could live long, sadly. But I'm glad he made it home.'

She had stayed for another day in Nerja with Jaime and then, with money he had lent her and which she had since repaid, she had taken a bus back to Málaga, where she had been ever since. She had trained as a nurse and was working in a local hospital. She loved the work and she had been happy living with Doña Rosalía.

'And Sister Encarnata?'

'She comes to visit from time to time. She's well. We always talk about you and try to imagine your life.'

Isabel had not seen or heard from her parents again but knew from her aunt in Madrid that her mother had died. Her voice quavered when she spoke of her mother. 'That was a bad time for me. I felt I should have been with her.'

'I still feel guilty that you had to leave her.'

'You shouldn't. It was my choice.'

They sat for a while in silence while Nick pondered how to raise the next subject. Isabel was gazing straight ahead, out to sea, and he remembered how often he had not been able to tell what she was thinking. He had talked to his mother about it and she had said that no one should expect to know everything another person was thinking. Their privacy had to be respected.

He decided to plunge in. 'I thought you might have married?'

'I was engaged for a while.' Isabel shrugged. 'Then I realised I had made a mistake, so I broke it off. I couldn't go through with it. After that, you know how it is in Spain, no man would want me.'

'I want you,' he said in a low voice.

'You feel obliged to.'

'No! It's got nothing to do with you saving my life or leaving your home to come with me.'

'It must have something.'

'Well, perhaps. It showed me what you were. Courageous and generous.'

'You will swell my head if you go on!'

'Isabel,' he said, 'seven years ago I asked you if you would come to Scotland with me. You said you had no clothes. You said you couldn't earn your living. I have come back to ask you again. You've got clothes now. And they need nurses in Scotland.'

She let out a peal of laughter. 'In that case,' she said, turning to him, 'how can I refuse?'

The best in classic and

Jane Austen

Elizabeth Laird

Beverley Naidoo   Roddy Doyle

Robert Swindells

George Orwell

Charles Dickens

Charlotte Brontë

Jan Mark

Anne Fine

Anthony Horowitz